戦争と平和の岐路で
AT THE CROSSROADS OF WAR AND PEACE

英日対訳 新撰詩集
New and Selected Poems in English and Japanese

デイヴィッド・クリーガー
DAVID KRIEGER

訳 結城 文
Translated by Aya Yuhki

コールサック社

戦争と平和の岐路で
AT THE CROSSROADS OF WAR AND PEACE

英日対訳 新撰詩集
New and Selected Poems in English and Japanese

デイヴィッド・クリーガー
DAVID KRIEGER

訳　結城　文
Translated by Aya Yuhki

コールサック社
Coal Sack Publishing Company
Tokyo, Japan

"Humanity has entered a new era in which our technical prowess has brought us to a crossroads."
—— Pope Francis

人類は我々の技術が我々を岐路に立たせるという新しい時代に入った
——フランシス法王

CONTENTS

A Poem for the Crossroads   10

I   CHILDREN OF WAR

Children of War   16
Duck and Cover   16
To an Iraqi Child   20
Zaid's Misfortune   22
The Children of Iraq Have Names   24
Qana Street Scene   28
The Chorus of Children Sings   30
Message to Youth   32

II   WAR IS TOO EASY

War Is Too Easy   36
Little Changes   38
That Was Then, This Is Now   40
Similarities: 1914 and 2014   42
Reflections on a Tragic History   44
Rules of Engagement   48
Think and Think Again   50
Surrender   52
When the Killing Stops   54
Promises of Peace   56

III   THE DRUMS

The Drums   60
Guernica   62
The Great War   66

目　次

　　岐路の詩　11

I　戦争の子供たち
戦争の子供たち　17
潜って覆う　17
イラクの子供　21
ザイドの不幸　23
イラクの子供達には名前があった　25
クアナ通りの光景　29
子供達の歌うコーラス　31
若者へのメッセージ　33

II　戦争はあまりにも安易だ
戦争はあまりにも安易だ　37
少ししかない変化　39
それはあの時のこと　これは今のこと　41
類似点：1914年と2014年　43
悲劇的な歴史についての回想　45
交戦の法則　49
考えに考えよ　51
降伏　53
殺戮が終わった時　55
平和の約束　57

III　太鼓
太鼓　61
ゲルニカ　63
大戦　67

Mother to Daughter, Buchenwald 1944   68
Emperor Hirohito on a White Horse   70
Vietnam   72
Norman Morrison   76
Decision to Resume Bombing Hanoi   78
In Truth, We Are Bombing Ourselves   80
The Young Men with the Guns   82
Bulldozers   86
Bombing Gaza: A Pilot Speaks   88
Firing Squad   90
The Other Side   92
Twenty Years of War   94
Of Hawks and Drones   96
Archeology of War   98
War in a Time of Cowardice   98
Soldiers Fall   102
Oh, War   104

IV   EINSTEIN'S REGRET

Einstein's Regret   108
A Short History Lesson: 1945   110
August Mornings   112
Hiroshima   114
Forgive Me, Mother   116
Among the Ashes   118
Nagasaki   120
Echoes in the Sky   122
Eisenhower's View   124
Where Did the Victims Go?   126

母から娘へ　ブーヘンヴァルト強制収容所　1944年　69
白馬にまたがった裕仁（昭和）天皇　71
ベトナム　73
ノーマン・モリソン　77
ハノイ空爆再開の決定　79
実の事を言えば　我々は自分たちを爆撃しているのだ　81
銃を持った若者たち　83
ブルドーザー　87
ガザ爆撃：一人のパイロットが語った　89
銃殺隊　91
反対側　93
戦争の二十年　95
鷹とドローンについて　97
戦争の考古学　99
臆病な時代の戦争　99
兵士たちは倒れる　103
おお　戦争よ　105

IV　アインシュタインの悔い

アインシュタインの悔い　109
短い歴史のレッスン：1945年　111
八月の朝　113
ヒロシマ　115
お母さん　許して　117
灰のなかで　119
ナガサキ　121
空のこだま　123
アイゼンハワーの見解　125
犠牲者たちはどこへいったのか？　127

On Becoming Death   128

The Deep Bow of a *Hibakusha*   130

A Grandmother's Story   132

God Responded with Tears   134

The Four Seasons of Hiroshima   136

Testing Nuclear Weapons in the Marshall Islands   138

What Shall We Call the Bomb Dropped on Hiroshima?   140

When the Bomb Became Our God   142

Twelve Possible Names for World War III   144

The Merry-Go-Round   146

A Butterfly Blinked   148

V   A CONSPIRACY OF DECENCY

A Conspiracy of Decency   152

Today Is Not a Good Day for War   154

Worse Than the War   158

Standing with Pablo   160

I Refuse   162

The Doves Flew High   164

Wake Up!   166

The One-Hearted   168

Great Truth Has Great Silence   170

VI   FIFTY-ONE REASONS FOR HOPE

Fifty-one Reasons for Hope   174

Fukushima   178

Take Three Gifts on Your Journey   180

ABOUT THE AUTHOR   182

COMMENTARY   184

死神になること　129
被爆者の最敬礼　131
あるおばあさんの物語　133
神は涙をもって応えた　135
ヒロシマの四季　137
マーシャル群島での核兵器実験　139
ヒロシマに落ちた爆弾をなんと呼ぶべきか？　141
原爆が神になった日　143
十二の第三次世界大戦名予測　145
メリーゴーランド　147
蝶は目をぱちぱちさせた　149

V　礼儀正しき共謀

礼儀正しき共謀　153
今日は戦争をするのにいい日ではない　155
戦争より悪い　159
パブロとともに立つ　161
私は拒否する　163
鳩は高く飛んだ　165
目を覚ませ！　167
ひたむきな人々　169
偉大な真実は偉大な沈黙　171

VI　希望のための五十一の理由

希望のための五十一の理由　175
フクシマ　179
あなたの旅に三つのお土産をもっていってください　181

著者紹介　183
解　説　185

A Poem for the Crossroads

I would like to write a poem and nail it
to a stake at humanity's crossroads.
It would say: choose your path wisely.

It would say: this path we are on is far
too treacherous, a trap for the unwary
and complacent.

It would say: take down the gun pointed
at humanity's heart—enough of war,
enough of nuclear weapons, enough
of stumbling toward collective suicide.

It would say: enough homage to death—
choose life and be a citizen of the world.
It would say: be kinder than necessary.

It would certainly say: when it rains, the water
sinks into the Earth and the grass grows
toward the sun.

It would say: when the winds blow, the leaves
will flutter from the trees like butterflies.
It would remind us to stop and look at
the beauty around us.

岐路の詩

私は一篇の詩を書き
人類の岐路にたつ杭に打ちつけたい
賢明に道を選べとそれには書いてあるだろう

我々のいるこの道はあまりにも危険
うかつに自己満足していてはわなにはまると
それには書いてあるだろう

人間の心臓を狙った銃を下しなさい
──戦争はもうたくさん、核兵器はもうたくさん
集団自決をやりそこなうことなどもうたくさんと
それには書いてあるだろう

死の賛美などもうたくさん──
生を選び世界の市民となろうとそれには書いてあるだろう
もっともっと親切であれとそれには書いてあるだろう

雨が降れば水は地球にしみこみ
草は太陽にむかって成長すると
それにはたしかに書いてあるだろう

風が吹き木々の葉むらが蝶のように翻るとき
私たちに立ち止まって
自分の周りの美しさに見入ることを思い出させると
それには書いてあるだろう

It would say: this is Eden, but it needs care.
It would say: before you choose a path, think
about the people of the future.

It would say: make each moment of your time
on Earth matter.

It would say: choose the path of peace.

これはエデンだ　しかし配慮が必要
あなたが道を選ぶ前に　未来の人たちのことを考えなさいと
それには書いてあるだろう

あなたが生きているどの瞬間をも大切にしなさいと
それには書いてあるだろう

平和の道を選びなさいとそれには書いてあるだろう

I

CHILDREN OF WAR

戦争の子供たち

Children of War

In war, children die,
float away on clouds of grief.
By far, the greatest lie of all
is the well-worn but absurd belief
that war is noble, not a crime.

In war, children writhe in pain,
while their parents wail.
Before we spread war's red stain,
should we not consider how we fail
the young, again and yet again?

Duck and Cover
circa 1950

Children,
this is the way you will be saved
from a nuclear attack. At the sound
of the bell you will scramble as fast
as you can under your desk,
facing downward toward the floor
in a kneeling position

戦争の子供達

戦争で子供達は死に
悲しみの雲にのって漂い去った
あらゆるものの中で飛びぬけて巨大な虚偽は
戦争は高貴なもので犯罪でないという
使い古された、しかしばかばかしい信念なのである

戦争で子供達は苦痛でのたうち
彼等の両親も声をあげて泣く
我々が戦争の赤い染みを塗りひろげる前に
いかに若者たちを繰り返し　繰り返し
見殺しにしているかを考えないのだろうか？

潜って覆う
1950年頃

子供達よ
これが核攻撃から
あなたを守る方法です
ベルの音で先を争って誰よりも早く
机の下にもぐり
ひざまずいた姿勢で床に顔をつけ
頭を両腕の上に置く

with your head resting on your arms.
Keep your eyes squeezed
tightly shut, not opening them
or looking up until you hear me say
"All clear."

This is the way you will be saved
from shards of glass and other objects
traveling at speeds of hundreds of miles
per hour. And from the flash of white
light that could melt your eyeballs. And
from the explosion that could scramble
your brains and the rest of your organs.
And this is the way you will be saved
from the fire that may incinerate you,
leaving you shriveled, charred
and lifeless.

This is the way you will be saved
from the radiation that will cause your gums
to bleed, your hair to fall out, leukemia
to form in your blood, and lead
to either a rapid and painful death,
or one more slow and painful.
Pay close attention to these directions
so you will get it right the first time.

両眼を引き絞り
しっかりと閉じ
「空襲警報解除」
と私がいうのを聞くまで
目を開いたり上をむいてはいけません

これが時速何百マイルの速度で
飛んでくるガラスの破片やその他の物体から
あなたを守る方法です
そしてあなたの眼球を
溶かすこともできる白い閃光から
あなたを守る方法です
そしてあなたの脳やその他の器官を粉々にする
爆発からあなたを守る方法です
そしてこれがあなたを焼き捨て　縮ませ　炭化し
命なきものとする火災から
あなたを守る方法です

これがあなたの歯茎から
出血し　頭髪が抜け落ち
あなたの血液に白血病を引き起こし
急速な苦痛に満ちた死に至らしめる
あるいはまた緩慢でもっと苦痛に満ちた死に至らしめる
放射能からあなたを守る方法です
これらの指示に周到な注意をはらいなさい
そうすればあなたは初めて正しく理解するでしょう

To an Iraqi Child
for Ali Ismail Abbas

So you wanted to be a doctor?

It was not likely that your dreams
would have come true anyway.

We didn't intend for our bombs to find you.

They are smart bombs, but they didn't know
that you wanted to be a doctor.

They didn't know anything about you
and they know nothing of love.

They cannot be trusted with dreams.

They only know how to find their targets
and explode in fulfillment.

They are gray metal casings with violent hearts,
doing only what they were created to do.

It isn't their fault that they found you.

Perhaps you were not meant to be a doctor.

イラクの子供
アリ イスマル アバスへ

それでは君は医師になりたいのだね？

兎も角も君の夢が実現することは
ありそうもないことだ

我々の爆弾が君を見つけるなど意図していないよ

我々の爆弾は頭がいいが
君が医師になりたがっていることは知らないよ

我々の爆弾は　君のことを何も知らないし
愛など何も知らないよ

夢なんていうものについて我々の爆弾を信用してはいけない

我々の爆弾は　いかにターゲットを見つけ
爆発を遂行するかを知っているだけだ

我々の爆弾は　凶暴な心を持った灰色の金属製で
製造された目的通りのことをするだけだ

我々の爆弾が君を見つけたとしても　かれらのせいではないよ

多分君が医師になれる筈でなかっただけさ

Zaid's Misfortune

Zaid had the misfortune
of being born in Iraq, a country
rich with oil.

Iraq had the misfortune
of being invaded by a country
greedy for oil.

The country greedy for oil
had the misfortune of being led
by a man too eager for war.

Zaid's misfortune multiplied
when his parents were shot down
in front of their medical clinic.

Being eleven and haunted
by the deaths of your parents
is a great misfortune.

In Zaid's misfortune
a distant silence engulfs
the sounds of war.

ザイドの不幸

ザイドは　石油の豊富な国
イラクに生まれたという
不運をもっていた

イラクは　石油にたいして
貪婪な国に侵略されるという
不運をもっていた

石油にたいして貪婪な国は
ひどく戦争をしたがっている男に
率いられているという不運をもっていた

ザイドの不幸は　彼の両親が
彼らの医療クリニックの前で射殺された時
倍増した

十一歳であったこと　両親の死の思い出に
とりつかれていたことは
大きな不幸であった

ザイドの不幸だったことは
遠い静寂が戦争の物音を
呑みこんでしまったことだった

The Children of Iraq Have Names

The children of Iraq have names.
They are not the nameless ones.

The children of Iraq have faces.
They are not the faceless ones.

The children of Iraq do not wear Saddam's face.
They each have their own face.

The children of Iraq have names.
They are not all called Saddam Hussein.

The children of Iraq have hearts.
They are not the heartless ones.

The children of Iraq have dreams.
They are not the dreamless ones.

The children of Iraq have hearts that pound.
They are not meant to be statistics of war.

The children of Iraq have smiles.
They are not the sullen ones.

The children of Iraq have twinkling eyes.
They are quick and lively with their laughter.

イラクの子供達には名前があった

イラクの子供達には名前があった
彼等は名もなき者達ではない

イラクの子供達には顔があった
彼等は顔なき者達ではない

イラクの子供達はサダムの顔をしていない
彼等は自分自身の顔をもっている

イラクの子供達には名前があった
彼等はみんなサダム・フセインと呼ばれているのではない

イラクの子供達には心があった
彼等は無情な者達ではない

イラクの子供達には夢があった
彼等は夢のない者達ではない

イラクの子供達には強く打つ心臓があった
彼等は戦争の統計となるべき者達ではない

イラクの子供達には笑顔があった
彼等は陰気な者達ではない

イラクの子供達には輝く瞳があった
彼等は機敏でよく笑い溌剌としていた

The children of Iraq have hopes.
They are not the hopeless ones.

The children of Iraq have fears.
They are not the fearless ones.

The children of Iraq have names.
Their names are not collateral damage.

What do you call the children of Iraq?
Call them Omar, Mohamed, Fahad.

Call them Marwa and Tiba.
Call them by their names.

イラクの子供達には希望があった
彼等は希望をもたない者達ではない

イラクの子供達には恐怖があった
彼等は怖れ知らずの者達ではない

イラクの子供達には名前があった
それらの名前には付随的な損害はない

イラクの子供達を何と呼びますか？
オマール、モハメッド、ファハドと呼びなさい

彼等をマルワ、チバと呼びなさい
彼等を彼等の名で呼びなさい

Qana Street Scene

"And the blood of children ran through the streets."
——Pablo Neruda

There are scenes too horrible
to imagine or dream. Yes, this is our world.
We slaughter infants in our wars in the most
gruesome ways. No need to leave such horror
to our imaginations. It plays on the nightly news.

Soldiers rarely kill infants on purpose.
It just happens. Soldiers are clumsy
at their craft, as are politicians at theirs.
Rather than diplomacy, soldiers fire rockets
and drop bombs from the blue sky.

There is blood on our hands, blood all around.
Small, thin arms stream blood. Blood flows
from collapsed lungs. There is nowhere
to hide, nowhere to play, nowhere to pray
and no redemption left.

クアナ通りの光景

「そして子供達の血は道という道に流れた」
　　　　　　　　　　――パブロ　ネルダ*

想像や夢想を絶する残酷な
場面があった　そうなのだ　これが私達の世界なのだ
我々は赤子達を戦争で最も身の毛のよだつやり方で
虐殺した　そうした恐怖を想像力に委ねる
必要はない　夜のニュースでやっている

兵士達は滅多に赤子達をわざと殺しはしない
それはたまたま起こってしまったのだ　兵士達は
政治家達と同様やり方が不器用なのだ
かけひきというより彼等はロケットを発射し
青空から爆弾を落とすのだ

我々の手は血に塗れ　血はあたり一面にとびちった
小さな　痩せた手から血は流れ　血は
破れた肺からも流れた　隠れるところなどなく
遊ぶところも　祈るところもないのだ
救済など残されていない

　　　　　　　　　　　　　＊チリの国民的詩人

The Chorus of Children Sings

Your bombs make such loud noise.
They hurt our hearts. They tear us apart.
Your bombs are powerful, but so are our hearts.

We only want to live as children.
We are sick of the bombs you drop on us.
Will you stop? Will you ever stop?

子供達の歌うコーラス

あんたたちの爆弾はあんなにも大きな音をたてる
私達の心を傷つけ　引き裂く
あんたたちの爆弾は強力だが　私達の心も強いよ

私達はただ子供として生きたいと願っているだけだ
私達はあんたたちの落とす爆弾にうんざりだ
止めてくれない？　本当に止めてくれない？

Message to Youth

You are not required
to kill on command, to wear
a uniform, to camouflage yourself,
to place medals on your chest, to check
your conscience at the door, to march
in unison, to bear the burden of the body count.

You are not required
to pledge allegiance to the flag, to sing
patriotic songs, to distort history,
to believe lies, to support leaders when
they are wrong, to turn a blind eye
to violence, or to be cheerleaders for war.

You are required
to love, to live with compassion, to be kinder
than necessary and to seek the truth
in the time allotted to you.

若者へのメッセージ

貴方たちは　命令で殺すこと
軍服を着ること　自分自身をごまかすこと
勲章を胸につけること　ドアのところで
良心をチェックすること
一斉行進をすること　死体の数勘定の重荷に
耐えることなどを要求されていない

貴方たちは　国旗に忠誠を誓うこと
愛国的な歌を歌うこと　歴史を歪めること
虚偽を信ずること　間違っていると
分かっている時もリーダーを支持すること
暴力から目をそむけること　戦争のチアリーダーに
なることなど要求されていない

貴方たちは
愛すること　優しさをもって生活し
十二分に親切で　貴方たちの生きている時代における
真理を追究することが要求されている

II

WAR IS TOO EASY

戦争はあまりにも安易だ

War Is Too Easy

If politicians had to fight the wars
they would find another way.

Peace is not easy, they say.
But it is war that is too easy—

too easy to turn a profit, too easy
to believe there is no choice,

too easy to sacrifice
someone else's children.

Someday it will not be this way.
Someday we will teach our children

that they must not kill,
that they must have the courage

to live peace, to stand firmly
for justice, to say no to war.

Until we teach our children peace
each generation will have its wars,

will find its own ways
to believe in them.

戦争はあまりにも安易だ

もしも政治家達が戦争をしなければならないとしたら
他の方法を見つけただろう

平和は容易ではないといわれるが
だから戦争をするというのはあまりにも安易だ

利益を得られる　他に選択肢がないと
信じるのはあまりにも安易だ

誰か他人の子供を犠牲にするのは
あまりにも安易だ

いつかこうしたやり方でなくなるだろう
いつか自分達の子供達に教えることになるだろう

人を殺してはいけないことを
勇気をもたなくてはいけないことを

平和に生きなければならないことを　正義にたいして
しっかりと立つこと　戦争にたいしてノーということを

我々が子供達に平和を教えるまで
それぞれの世代には　戦争が起こるだろう

しかし自分達の信じる
それぞれの方法を見つけることだろう

Little Changes

Our brave young soldiers
shot babies at My Lai—
few remember.

Lieutenant Calley—
sentenced to house arrest
until pardoned by Nixon.

Then it was *gooks*.
Now it is *hajjis*—
little changes.

Abu Ghraib—
the buck stops nowhere.
It still hasn't stopped.

From My Lai
to Abu Ghraib—
the terrible silence.

少ししかない変化

我が国の勇敢な若い兵士達が
ソンミ村*1で赤ん坊を撃ったことを
覚えている人は少ない

カーリー中尉*2――
ニクソンに許されるまで
自宅監禁になった

それから グック*3 となり
今は ハッジ*4――
少ししかない変化

アブグレイブ刑務所*5――
跳ねあがりは止らない
それはまだ止まっていない

ソンミ村から
アブグレイブ刑務所まで――
身の毛のよだつ沈黙

＊1：1968年アメリカ兵が数百人の非武装のベトナム人を虐殺した
＊2：その事件の責任者
＊3：アメリカ兵がベトナム人を蔑んで呼んだ語
＊4：アメリカ兵がイラク人を蔑んで呼んだ語
＊5：アメリカ軍がイラク人拘留者を収容したイラクの刑務所

That Was Then, This Is Now

"We had to destroy the village to save it."
—— An American Colonel

We had to destroy the village
the whole damn village
every last living soul
every thatched roof hut
every stick, every stone
to save it.

That was then.

We had to destroy the world
the whole damn world
every high rise
every thatched roof hut
every living thing
that walks, that crawls, that flies
that laughs, that sings, that cries
to save it.

This is now.

それはあの時のこと　これは今のこと

「我々はその村を破壊しなくてはならない　それを救うために」
　　　　　　　　　　　　——あるアメリカ軍大佐

　　我々はその村を破壊しなくてはならない
　　あのいまいましい村全体を
　　すべての最後まで生き残った者ども
　　すべての藁葺屋根の小屋を
　　すべての柱　石を
　　それを救うために

　　それはあの時のことだった

　　我々は世界を破壊しなくてはならない
　　あのいまいましい世界全体を
　　すべての高く盛り上がったものを
　　すべての藁葺屋根の小屋を
　　歩き　這い　飛び
　　笑い　歌い　叫ぶ
　　すべての生き物を破壊しなくてはならない
　　それを救うために

　　これは今のことである

Similarities: 1914 and 2014

The countries of Europe, it is said,
stumbled into World War I, a war
no one wanted and yet, and yet...it happened.
After Archduke Franz Ferdinand's assassination,
it became the Great War, taking the lives
of a generation of young men too eager to fight
in the battlefield trenches.

What can we say about the confrontation
of great powers, going on at this very moment,
in Ukraine? Could the leaders of these countries
be stumbling again, this time on a powder
keg of nuclear alliance, misunderstandings,
irrationality, false promises, political realities
and unrealities, indignation and, above all,
bravado, as always, bravado for God and country?

類似点：1914年と2014年

ヨーロッパの国々は
第一次大戦——誰も望まなかった　それなのに
それにもかかわらず起こってしまった戦争に
よろめき込んだといわれている
フランツ・フェルディナンド大公の暗殺後
大戦になり　戦場の塹壕で戦うことを
あまりにも熱望する若者世代の命を奪った

我々は　ウクライナで現におきている
大国間の対決について　なんといったら
いいのだろう？　これらの国の指導者は
今回は核同盟の火薬樽に　また　つまづくのか？
意見の不一致　不合理性　虚偽の約束
政治的現実や非現実　憤り　そして
なによりもまずブラボー
いつものように神と国にたいしてのブラボーなのか？

Reflections on a Tragic History

From sea to shining sea, across the continent,
how can our hearts not be broken in America?

Our Founding Fathers, even those who spoke
of "unalienable rights," were slaveholders.

Riches were amassed on the broken lives
and welted backs of slaves.

In an early act of genocide, we gave
germ-infested blankets to the Indians.

We forced these native peoples onto reservations
and took their lands.

When it came to modern war, we carpet bombed cities,
massacring civilians.

We created atomic weapons and obliterated
Hiroshima and Nagasaki for all the wrong reasons.

We sacrificed our children and slaughtered peasants
for presidential lies.

悲劇的な歴史についての回想

海から輝く海に向かって　大陸を横切り
我々の心はアメリカにあって破れないのか？

「譲りわたすことのできない権利」を語る
我々の建国者たちも奴隷所有者であった

富は奴隷たちの命や鞭打たれた背中と
引き換えに蓄えられた

初期の虐殺の行為として　我々は
インディアン達に細菌に汚染された毛布を与えた

我々は　先住民達を指定保留地へ
追い込み　かれらの土地を奪った

近代戦になると　都市を絨毯爆撃し
市民を虐殺した

我々は　原子兵器を製造し　誤った理由のために
ヒロシマ　ナガサキを壊滅させた

我々は　大統領の嘘のために
我々の子供を犠牲にし　多くの農夫達を殺した

We invaded and occupied countries and destroyed lives too numerous to count.

We bestowed medals, sang patriotic songs and wrote glorious histories.

Is there no possibility that our hearts, like sad continents, may reattach themselves to life?

我々は　他国を侵略し　占領し
数えきれないほど多くの命を奪った

我々は　勲章を授与し　国歌を歌い
栄光の歴史を書いた

我々の心が　悲しい大陸のように
命に再び立ち還る可能性はないのだろうか？

Rules of Engagement

"Golden like a shower."
————US Marine

Three Afghan men lay dead on their backs in the dirt.
Above them, four US Marines in battle gear celebrate
by urinating on them. These young Marines
with their golden showers are holding up a mirror
to America. It reminds us: *this is who we are.*

When we teach our children to kill we turn them
into something we don't understand: ourselves.
Their lack of humanity is not different from ours.
We have not taught these young men to value life,
but they are teaching us how little we do.

Why should they hold back when we have
taught them and sent them to kill other men—
men whose names they will never know?
If we are shocked by their disrespect for the dead,
we should consider our own for the living.

交戦の法則

　　　　「黄金のシャワーのごとく」
　　　　　　——アメリカ海兵隊員

三人のアフガン人が死んで泥の上に仰向けに倒れていた
それに向かって軍隊装備の四人のアメリカ海兵隊員が
放尿をして浮かれ騒いでいた　黄金のシャワーで祝った
彼ら若い海兵隊員たちは　アメリカに鏡を突きつける
我々に「これが我々なんだ」と気づかせる

我々が自分たちの子供たちに殺すことを教える時
彼らを理解できない何かに変えてしまう　我々自身をもだ
彼らの人間性の欠如は　我々も同じだ
我々は若者たちに命を尊重することを教えなかったが
彼らは　我々がいかに教えなかったかを教える

名前も知らぬ他者を殺すことを教え送りだしておいて
何故彼らは自制しなければならないのか
彼らの死者にたいする無礼さに衝撃を受けるなら
我々自身が生きている者にしていることを
考えてみる必要があるだろう

Think and Think Again

In the revolution, men fought
for cause and country, not for a lie.

In the Great War, they say
the best young men followed the flag,
fought in the trenches and died
on the barbed-wire fields of battle.
A generation was more than lost.
It was destroyed.

In our generation
the bravest young men went to prison
and served their time. They refused
to salute, carry a rifle, and kill peasants
in jungles on the far side of the world.

The worst of our generation also refused
to fight. They gathered deferments
until they could walk away in safety.
Strange that these are the ones,
the Cheneys, who found old ways
to bring new generations to war.

Young men, learn history and think
and think again. Too many have died,
not for cause and country, but for a lie.

考えに考えよ

革命において　男たちは
主義や国のために闘った　虚偽のためではない

大戦において　最も優秀な若者たちは
国旗に従い　塹壕で戦い
鉄条網のある戦場で戦死したといわれている
一つの世代が失われたというより
破壊されてしまったのだ

我々の世代では
最も勇敢な若者たちは　牢獄へゆき
服役した　彼らは敬礼し
ライフルを担ぎ　遠い世界のジャングルで
農民たちを殺すことを拒否したのだ

また　我々の世代で最悪だった者たちは
戦うのを拒否した　彼らは安全に逃れ去るまで
徴兵猶予を幾度もつかった
彼らが新しい世代を戦争に駆り立てる
古くからのやり方をする
チェイニー一派*だったのはおかしいことだ

若者たちよ　歴史を学びなさい　そして
考えに考えなさい　あまりにも多くの者が
主義や国のためでなく　虚偽のために死んでいるのだ

＊元副大統領ディック・チェイニーのような好戦的人物

Surrender

The barbarians swept past the crumbled city walls,
seizing the highest offices in the land. They rang
the temple bells, but we were deaf to the alarm.

They trained our children in the arts of war
and ferried them to distant lands. Like tin soldiers,
like dominoes the young soldiers tipped and fell.

Promises fell faster than our youth but no one
raised a voice.

Forgotten now is Orwell, who warned of darkening skies.
Forgotten now is Gandhi, who quietly held his ground.
Forgotten now is King, who thundered out his dream.

降伏

野蛮人たちはその国の最高機関を占領すると
崩れた都市の壁を過去へおしやった　彼らは
寺院の鐘を鳴らしたが　我々は警鐘には耳をかさなかった

彼らは我々の子供たちに戦争の技術を教え
遠い国へフェリーで送った　鉛の兵隊のように
ドミノのように　若い兵士たちはよろめき倒れた

約束は若者たちよりも早く崩れ落ちた　だが
誰も声をあげない

今や　暗くなってゆく空を警告したオーウェルは　忘れられた
今や　しずかに自分の立場を保持しようとしたガンジーは　忘れられた
今や　自分の夢を大声で叫んだキングも　忘れられた

When the Killing Stops

When the killing stops
we declare victory
without weighing the bitterness.

We will not regain our humanity
by pinning medals on those
who pulled the triggers.

We will not find our lost souls
while we prepare
for our next onslaught.

Our army is powerful.
It bombs, it maims, it kills.
But where has our humanity gone?

殺戮が終わった時

殺戮が終わった時
我々は辛苦の重さを量ることなく
勝利を宣言する

引き金を引いた者たちに
勲章をつけさせることで
我々の人間性を取り戻すことはできない

来るべき殺戮を
準備している者たちに
失った魂を見つけることはできない

我々の軍隊は強力だ
爆撃し　戦傷を負わせ　殺す
けれど　我々の人間性は一体どこへいってしまったのか？

Promises of Peace

The last century, a monument to war,
Keeps marching into the future.
Fathers don't know what to tell their sons,
But the dull leader knows:
>*Find the enemy and kill him.*

And *him* may be a mother or her sweet child.
Patriotic words always mean that someone soon
Will die. It's carved in solemn stone.
The bombs don't calculate, they only
>*Seek the enemy to kill.*

There is no beauty in war, nor decency, nor
Wisdom. There is only force and blind obedience.
Bombs fall, children die and generals are celebrated.
In the public square new names, new sacrifice.
>*Promises of peace give way to war.*

平和の約束

前世紀　戦争を讃える記念碑が
未来に向けて行進し始めた
父たちは息子たちにいうべき言葉を知らなかった
しかし　なまくらな指導者は知っていた：
　　　　　　　敵を見つけ殺せ

そして多分 *彼* には母があり　彼はその可愛い息子かもしれなかった
愛国的な言葉は常に誰かがまもなく死ぬだろうということを
意味している　それは荘重に石に彫られる
爆弾は忖度しない　ただ
　　　　　　　殺す敵を求めているのだ

戦争には美も　礼儀も
叡智もない　そこには軍隊と盲従があるだけだ
爆弾は落ち　子供たちは死に　そして将官は顕彰される
公共広場には　新しい名前　新しい犠牲
　　　　　　平和の約束は戦争に屈する

III

THE DRUMS

太鼓

The Drums

They're beating on the drums again,
the drums, the drums.
They're calling out the young men again,
young men, young men.

They're training them to kill again,
with knives and guns,
with tanks and bombs.

They're sending them away again,
across the ocean
by ship, by plane.

They're acting up at home again,
the mothers, the mothers.
They don't want their sons to go again
to die, to die.

And now they're coming home again
in caskets wrapped in flags
with shrapnel in their backs,
with heroin in their veins.

And now they're coming home again
with snickers on their lips,
with medals on their chests.

太鼓

彼らはまた太鼓をたたきだした
太鼓　太鼓
彼らはまた若者たちを召集しはじめた
若者たち　若者たち

彼らはまた殺す訓練をはじめた
ナイフと銃で
タンクと爆弾で

彼らはまた派兵しようとしている
海を越えて
船で　飛行機で

彼らはまた国内で行動しはじめた
お母さんたち　お母さんたち
彼女らはまた自分の息子たちが
死にに　死ににゆくのを望まない

そして今や彼らはまた故国へ帰ってきた
旗に包まれた棺のなかで
背中に砲弾の破片
血管にはヘロインをもって

そして今や彼らはまた故国へ帰ってきた
口元には忍び笑いを
胸には勲章をつけて

They're blowing on the bugles now.
They're beating on the drums,
the drums, the drums.

Guernica

Nazi Luftwaffe bombs fall
on a small Basque village.
It is market day.
The streets are jammed.

Nazis bomb and strafe.
Planes dive, machine guns fire.
The young Luftwaffe pilots
find the marketplace.

Villagers and peasants
run for their lives
as death blurts from the sky.
Seventeen hundred murdered and maimed.

Picasso shares his human outrage
in his unforgettable *Guernica*,
the Guernica of screams and death.
Fallen man, fallen horse.

今や彼らはラッパを吹いている
彼らは太鼓をたたいている
太鼓　太鼓を

ゲルニカ

ナチ　ドイツ空軍の爆弾は
小さなバスクの村に落ちた
市場の立つ日で
通りは人でいっぱいだった

ナチは爆撃し機銃掃射をした
飛行機は低空飛行し　マシンガンは火を噴いた
ドイツ空軍の若いパイロットは
市場を見つけた

村人や行商人たちは
だしぬけに死が空から降ってきたので
命からがらに逃げた
千七百人が殺され　不具になった

ピカソは彼の不朽の名作
叫喚と死の　ゲルニカ　で
彼の人間としての憤怒を共にした
倒れる人　倒れる馬

Bland bureaucrats may try to hide
this Guernica
to protect the shameless ones
who thunder for more war.

But Guernica cannot so easily
be put aside: Cover *Guernica*
and its power breaks through.
Starker, stronger, truer.

For those who would make war
Guernica was painted for you.

いんぎんな官僚たちは
このゲルニカを隠そうとするかもしれない
大声で戦争を推進しようとする
恥知らずの者どもを保護するために

しかしゲルニカはそんなに簡単に
片付けられるものではない──　ゲルニカを覆えば
その力はカバーを突き抜ける
もっと赤裸々に　もっと強く　もっと真実に

戦争を企む者ども
お前たちのために　ゲルニカ は描かれたんだ

The Great War

They thought it would be just another war, to be won
or lost, not one of stench and standoff in the deadly fields
and trenches, beneath an anguished sun.

They thought the boys would be home in months, not years,
but time dragged on in nightmarish charges against barbwire
and machineguns, stoking terrible fears.

When the war began, no one could foresee the cost,
but on the battlefields of Europe a generation fought and died
or, traumatized, lost their minds; a generation was lost.

Years after the Great War's slaughter was finally done,
it would take an even more expansive and more deadly war
before the Great War would be called World War I.

From where we stand, it may be hard to clearly see
how our hubris and our weaponry of mass annihilation
have set us on a tragic course for World War III.

大戦

勝とうと敗れようと　苦悶している太陽の下
激戦地や塹壕での死臭や冷淡さといったものとは別の
戦争になるだろうと思った

少年たちは何年というのでなく　何カ月で帰国できると思っていた
しかし　期間は延長し　有刺鉄線やマシンガンへの
悪夢のような突撃命令となってすさまじい恐怖をつのらせた

戦争が始まった時　誰もコストを予見できなかった
しかしヨーロッパの戦場では　一つの世代が戦って死んだ
さもなければ　精神的外傷を受け　正気を失い　一つの世代が失われた

大戦の殺戮が最終的に終わって何年もして
その大戦が第一次大戦と呼ばれるまでに
もっと広範囲でもっと致命的な戦争があった

我々のたっているところから　我々の傲慢さと大量絶滅の武器庫が
第三次世界大戦の悲劇的なコースに我々をおいているかを
はっきり見きわめることはむつかしいのかもしれない

Mother to Daughter, Buchenwald 1944

Child, the world will be the world again.

Hold tight to this thought, embrace it.
The bitter grayness of senseless death
will not last forever.

Water the tree of hope with your tears.
Child, the fruit of this tree grows
even in darkness.

One day this fruit will be ready to harvest.
On that day, in the magic of life, this place
will be as distant as the stars.

母から娘へ　ブーヘンヴァルト強制収容所[*]　1944年

わが子よ　世界は再び元の世界になるでしょう

この考えをしっかりと持ちなさい　それを抱きしめなさい
無意味な死の苦々しい灰色は
永久には続かない

希望の木にあなたの涙を注ぎなさい
わが子よ　この木の果実は
暗闇でも育つ

いつかかの実は収穫できるようになるでしょう
その日　人生の魔術で　この場所は
星のように遠くなるでしょう

＊ナチス・ドイツの強制収容所

Emperor Hirohito on a White Horse

"I swallow my own tears..."
———Emperor Hirohito

Surrender has a bitter taste.

Even in this old photograph at the height of empire,
sitting straight on a white horse in his imperial uniform,
a sash across his torso, his sword by his side,
with war medals glittering on his chest,
he appears small and vulnerable.

Emperors and fools leave little space for defeat.

He dismounts from the white horse, carefully puts away
the imperial uniform, the sash, the sword, the medals.

He sits quietly, alone, contemplating the small cup
of tears, as though the cup were filled with hemlock.

白馬にまたがった裕仁（昭和）天皇

　　「私は涙を呑む」
　　　　――天皇 裕仁

降伏は苦い味であった

帝国という高さにあった古い写真においてさえ
白馬に直立してまたがり　礼服をつけ
胴には肩章、脇には剣
胸には戦功の勲章を光らせていても
小さく　弱弱しかった

天皇たちや愚か者どもはまもなく敗北した

彼は白馬から降り　注意深く
礼服　肩章　剣　勲章を片付けた

彼は静かに座り　一人だけで　小さな涙のカップを
見つめた　あたかもそれが毒人参の液でみたされているように

Vietnam

In the 1960s, they gave us our own war, not
too big a war and not too small, a war that seemed
to them just the right size for escalation.

The war came complete with a country to invade,
jungles, real and artificial leaders, and small brown
people who wanted to be free.

They used the draft to hijack us from our youth,
gave us promises and lies, boots and uniforms,
weapons and military training.

The military taught us to shout "Kill, kill, kill,"
as we lunged with bayonets at imaginary enemies,
as we filled our hearts with sadness.

Unfortunately, the country they gave us for war
was on the other side of the world, a place covered
with dark jungles, humid and thick.

Even more unfortunate, the small brown people
didn't seem to want our help, already having their
own leaders and preferring their own path to freedom.

ベトナム

1960年代に　彼等は我々に我々自身の戦争を与えた
大きすぎるのでなく　小さすぎるのでもなく　エスカレートするに
ちょうどいい規模の戦争のように彼らには思えた

その戦争は侵略する国　ジャングル
現実のそして人為的な指導者と　自由であることを求める
小柄な褐色の人たちで完璧なものになった

彼らは青春時代から我々をハイジャックするために徴兵し
我々に約束と虚偽　ブーツとユニフォーム
武器と軍事訓練を与えた

軍隊は我々に「殺せ　殺せ　殺せ」と叫ぶことを教えた
仮想の敵に銃剣で突進するように
心を悲しみでいっぱいにするように

不幸なことに　彼らが我々に戦争を与えた国は
世界の反対側にあり　暗いジャングルに覆われた場所で
湿度が高く　どんよりとしたところだった

もっと不幸だったことは　その小柄な褐色の人たちは
我々の助力を望んでいないようだった　すでに自分たちの
指導者がおり　自由への彼ら自身の道を好んでいるようだった

We bombed them with napalm and chased them
through the jungles until they died, or disappeared
to fight another day.

Our leaders kept on giving. They gave us nightly
body counts, a measure of success that there were more
of them who died than us.

When the war was over, they gave us a polished black
granite wall in Washington DC, with the names
of the 58,195 Americans who died in the war.

At the wall, we can see our reflections and reflect
upon the war they gave us, their promises and lies,
and the terrible waste of it all.

我々はやつらをナパーム弾で爆撃し　ジャングルのなかを
やつらが死ぬまで　あるいは後で戦うために
消えるまで　やつらを追いかけた

我々のリーダーは負けつづけた　彼らは毎晩
死体を数えさせた　我々よりやつらの方が
多く死んだというのを成功の目安とするために

戦争が終わったとき　彼らはワシントンＤＣに
その戦争で死んだ58,195名のアメリカ人の名前を彫った
黒御影石の磨いた壁を　我々に贈ってくれた

我々はその壁に自分たちを回想し彼らが
我々にあたえた戦争について熟慮する　彼らの約束と虚偽
そしてすべての恐るべき浪費について反省する

Norman Morrison
November 2, 1965

Sitting calmly before the Pentagon, like a Buddhist monk,
he doused himself in kerosene, lit a match and went up in flame.

I imagine McNamara, stiff and unflinching, as he watched
from above.

To his wife, Morrison wrote, "Know that I love thee,
but I must go to help the children of the priest's village."

When it happened, the wife of the YMCA director said,
"I can understand a heathen doing that, but not a Christian."

Few Americans remember his name, but in Vietnam
children still sing songs about his courage.

ノーマン・モリソン
1965年11月2日

ペンタゴンの前に仏教の僧侶のように静かに坐り
灯油をかぶり　マッチを擦って　炎のなかで昇天した

マクナマラは上から見おろして
硬直し　断固としていたと想像する

モリソンは妻に「お前を愛していることは分かっているが
僧侶の村の子供たちを助けるために私はゆかねばならない」と書き残した

それがおきたとき　YMCAのディレクターの妻は言った
「異教徒がするなら分かるが　キリスト教徒のすることではない」

アメリカ人で彼の名を覚えている者は少ないが　ベトナムでは
今でも子供たちは彼の勇気を歌っている

Decision to Resume Bombing Hanoi

Aides uncoil from their desks
and slither down dark corridors.
Approaching the President
their tongues flick red
from thin, dry lips.

The President hisses lowly,
approvingly,
slips to his belly,
glides toward his aides
until they entwine,
their rattles shivering.

Their tongues quiver menacingly
until the decision is made;
then slowly they slide apart.

ハノイ空爆再開の決定

補佐官たちは机からほどかれ
暗い廊下を滑り下りた
大統領に近づくと
薄く　乾いた唇から
赤い舌が閃いた

大統領は不満げに低くしーっと言った
是認するように
自分の腹の方へ滑りこんだ
補佐官たちの方へ滑りこんだ
彼らが絡み合うまで
ガタガタ震えていた

決定がなされるまで
彼らの舌は威嚇的に震えていた
それからゆっくりと彼らはわかれた

In Truth, We Are Bombing Ourselves

Snails speak louder to truth
than our politicians speak to conscience,
and the voices of frogs are clearer yet than poets.

The truth which touches me across time and space
is risking all for life.

It flows in mother's milk,
echoes from the feet
of those who walked away, refusing to kill,
is carried on the backs of snails,
proclaimed in the voices of frogs
and knows no boundaries.

実の事を言えば　我々は自分たちを爆撃しているのだ

　　　我々の政治家たちが良心に話しかけるより
　　　もっと大きな声で　蝸牛たちは真実に話しかける
　　　そして蛙たちの声は　詩人たちの声より明晰だ

　　　時空を越えて私に触れてくる真実は
　　　生涯を通じて危害を蒙る危険がある

　　　それは母の乳に流れ
　　　殺すことを拒絶して歩み去る者たちの
　　　足から響き
　　　蝸牛たちの背中にのって運ばれ
　　　蛙たちの声で宣言され
　　　境界をしらない

The Young Men with the Guns
for Father Roy Bourgeois

"Let those who have a voice speak for the voiceless"
———Bishop Oscar Romero

None of it could have happened
not the killings, the rapes, the brutality
without the young men with the guns.

Bishop Romero saw this clearly.
Lay down your arms, he said.
This, the day before his assassination,

the day before they shot him at the altar.
God, forgive them, they only follow orders.
They know not what they do.

But the politicians and the generals
know what they do
when they give their orders
to murder at the altar.

None of it could have happened
not the killings, the rapes, the brutality
without the politicians and the generals.

銃を持った若者たち
ロイ・ブルジョワ神父[*1]のために

　　　「声をもつ者たちは声なき者たちのために話そう」
　　　　　　　　　——オスカル・ロメロ大司教[*2]

殺人も　レイプも　残虐行為も
銃を持った若者たちなしでは
決して起こらなかった

ロメロ司教はそれを明確に知っていた
「*武器を捨てなさい*」と彼は
暗殺される前の日にいった

彼が聖壇で撃たれる前に
「神よ　彼らを許したまえ　彼らは命令に従っているだけですから
　彼らは自分たちがしていることを知らないのですから」と言った

しかし政治家たちや将官たちは
聖壇で殺すという
命令をした時に
自分たちが何をしているのか知っていた

殺人も　レイプも　残虐行為も
政治家たちや将官たちなしでは
けっして起こらなかった

The ones who sit in dark rooms
and stuff their mouths with food
before they give the orders.

The people are silent.
Their mouths will not open.
They hang their heads and avert their eyes.

Of course, they are afraid
of the young men with the guns
who carry out the orders.

None of it could have happened
without the people remaining silent.

The Bishop staggered, he bled, he died.
But he will never be silenced.

暗い部屋に坐り
命令をする前に
口に食べ物を詰めこんだ者たち

民衆は静かだった
彼らの口は開かないだろう
彼らは頭を垂れ目をそらした

勿論　彼らは
命令を実行する
銃を持った若者たちを恐れていた

民衆が口を噤んでいることなしに
そうしたことは決して起こらなかった

司教はよろめき　血を流し　死んだ
しかし　決して彼の口は噤ませられないだろう

＊１　旧アメリカ陸軍学校に抗議したカソリック神父
＊２　サン・サルバドルのカソリック大司教

Bulldozers

In Desert Storm, an American war,
the U.S. military put bulldozer blades on its tanks
and buried Iraqi soldiers alive in desert sands.
This deserves more than a footnote in the annals
of human cruelty.

Rachel Corrie, a young American, stood
before an Israeli bulldozer that threatened the home
of a Palestinian family. She refused to give way.
This deserves more than a footnote in the annals
of human courage.

ブルドーザー

砂嵐のなかでのあるアメリカの戦
米軍はブルドーザーの刃をタンクにつけ
イラク兵を生きたまま砂漠の砂に埋めた
これは人間の残酷さをしめす記録のなかでも
脚注をつける以上に値する

若いアメリカ人のレイチェル・コリー*は
パレスチナ人の家を破壊しようとする
イスラエルのブルドーザーの前にたちはだかった
彼女は敗けなかった
これは人間の勇気をしめす記録のなかでも
脚注をつける以上に値する

*二十三歳のアメリカ平和活動家

Bombing Gaza: A Pilot Speaks

The stain of death spreads below,
but from my cockpit I see none of it.
I only drop bombs as I have been trained
and then, far above the haze and blood,
I speed toward home.

I am deaf to the screams of pain.
Nor can I smell the stench of slaughter.
I try not to think of children shivering
with fear or of those blown to pieces.

They tell me I am brave, but
how brave can it be to drop bombs
on a crowded city? I am a cog, only that,
a cog in a fancy machine of death.

ガザ爆撃：一人のパイロットが語った

死の染みは下で広がっているが
コックピットからは何も見えない
私は訓練されたように爆弾を落としただけだった
それから　靄と血のはるか上空を
急いで故国へむかった

私には苦痛の叫びは聞こえなかったし
虐殺の死臭も嗅がなかった
私は恐怖で震えている子供たちやバラバラに
吹き飛ばされた者たちのことを考えないようにした

私は勇敢だったと言われた　しかし
密集した都市に爆弾を落とすことが
どうして勇敢であり得よう　私は歯車の歯　それだけだ
死の極上機械の歯だったのだ

Firing Squad

Saddam Hussein is a bad man
So let's line up the children of Iraq
And shoot them.

Saddam is a very bad man
So let's line up the mothers of Iraq
And shoot them.

We know that Saddam is a bad man
So let's line up all the old people of Iraq
And shoot them.

Saddam is a very bad man
And firing squads are old fashioned
So let's just bomb Baghdad.

After we've bombed the Iraqis
With our "shock and awe" two-day plan
Surely they will welcome us as liberators.

Surely the Iraqis will praise Allah
That they have been so fortunate
To have been bombed with such precision.

銃殺隊

サダム・フセインは悪い奴だ
だからイラクの子供たちを整列させ
撃ち殺そう

サダム・フセインはとても悪い奴だ
だからイラクの母親たちを整列させ
撃ち殺そう

我々はサダム・フセインは悪い奴だと知っている
だからイラクの老人たちを整列させ
撃ち殺そう

サダム・フセインはとても悪い奴だ
銃殺隊はもう古い
そこでバグダッドを爆撃しよう

我々がイラクを「ショックを与え怖れさせる」という
二日がかりの計画で爆撃した後
確かに彼らは我々を解放者として歓迎するだろう

確かにイラク人たちはとても正確に爆撃が
おこなわれたので大変幸運だったと
アラーを讃えるだろう

Surely they will recognize
That their oil is better in our hands.
Saddam Hussein is a very bad man.

The Other Side

In this sacred place defined by water, gentle
breezes and the sounds of birds, a lone kayaker
paddles across the shimmering bay toward
the horizon. This is one side of the world.

On the other side, bombs drop on cities
blowing up children and other innocents
for the sake of vengeance or peace or
whatever reason. For the mothers

there is nothing but the cold terror
of the silver planes unloading
their lethal cargo, and the anguish
of losing those they love.

Young pilots and their crews
do with deadly precision only what
they were so well trained to do
on the other side of the world.

確かに彼らはかれらの石油が
我々の手にあることのほうがましだと認めるだろう
サダム・フセインはとても悪い奴だ

反対側

水で区切られたこの聖なる場所では
そよ風と小鳥のさえずり　水平線へ向かって
輝く湾を一艘のカヤックが櫂で横切ってゆく
これがこの世の一面だ

反対側では　都市に爆弾が落ち
子供や無実なものたちが
復讐　平和　その他の理由で
吹き飛ばされている

銀色の飛行機が致命的な
積荷を投下する時ほど母たちにとって
愛するものを失うという
冷たい恐怖に優るものはない

若いパイロットと乗員たちは
世界の反対側で　そんなにも十分に
訓練されたものすごい正確さで
遂行しただけだった

Twenty Years of War

Ours is a geography of fear, a world
of ghosts, interrogation rooms, corrupt
authorities and mingled bones.

As much as we may wish it, there is no
shining path. The space for withdrawal
or surrender narrows.

Sad trails wind up and down snow covered
mountains. In the weighty silence, the dead,
half-dead and tortured are ever present.

Gravity pulls on recurring nightmares,
as women hide trembling
behind thick walls and iron gates.

Shards of truth are unearthed, examined
and discarded. Old generals, defiant, brace
themselves to hold their bloody ground.

But the people, one by one, find courage
and each other in the streets. They rush
like water, against the fiery walls of war.

戦争の二十年

わが国は恐怖の地理学であり
幽霊の世界であり　疑問の部屋
腐敗した権力と入りまじった骨の世界である

どんなに我々が望もうとも
輝く道は望めない　退却と
降伏の空間は　狭まった

悲しみの道は冠雪の山々を巻くように
上ったり下ったりする　重々しい沈黙の中に　死者
死にかかった者　拷問にかけられた者たちがまだいる

重力はくりかえす悪夢を引き
女たちは震えながら
厚い壁や鉄の門の後に隠れる

真実の破片は明るみにだされ　調べられ
そして捨てられた　古い将官たちは挑戦的に
自分たちの血にまみれた根拠を保持しようとした

しかし民衆は　一人また一人と街で
勇気を見つけ　互いを見出し　水のように
戦争という炎の壁へと突進した

Of Hawks and Drones

A red-tailed hawk soars and circles
above the tall trees and silent fields
looking down for movement, for prey.
Gray clouds press against nearby mountains.
From another direction the sun lights up
the fields and mountainside.

Somewhere in an innocuous, but not innocent,
place in the United States of America,
a young military officer stares intently
at a computer screen. He operates
the remote control of a predator drone
flying softly above houses in Pakistan,
but it could be anywhere.

The young officer releases precision missiles
above the target he has been given. People die.

They are not always the right people. Sometimes
they are children. Sometimes the information
is wrong, the coordinates are mistaken.

The red-tailed hawk glides on currents of thin air,
then dives toward Earth, talons at the ready.

鷹とドローンについて

赤い尾をした鷹が高い樹木や
静かな野の上を飛翔し旋回しながら
動くもの　餌をみおろしていた
灰色の雲が近くの山脈におしかぶさっていた
反対側から太陽が
野原や山腹を照らしていた

アメリカ合衆国の無害だが、無罪とはいえない
どこかで　若い軍人が　熱心に
コンピューターの画面を見つめていた
彼はリモート・コントロールを操作して
パキスタンの家々の上に静かに
攻撃用ドローンを飛ばせていた
しかしそれはどこでもよかった

若い軍人は与えられた的に向かって
正確にミサイルを発射した　人々は死んだ

彼らはいつも正しい人たちとは限らない　時折り
彼らは子供だった　時々情報は間違う
連携を誤る

赤い尾をした鷹が薄い空気の流れの上を滑っていった
それから地上へと降下した　鉤爪は用意できている

Archeology of War

The years of war have numbed us,
grinding us down as they pile up one upon
the other forming a burial mound not only
for the fallen soldiers and innocents
who were killed, but for the parts of us,
once decent and bright with hope,
now deflated by the steady fall of death
and sting of empty promises.

War in a Time of Cowardice

Lessons Learned from Vietnam

Begin with lies, the bolder the better. Diagrams
are helpful.

Dump the draft. Promise the poor an education
after they serve.

Tell the people that the war will either save democracy
or spread it.

戦争の考古学

戦争の歳月は　我々を麻痺させた
倒れた兵士たちや　殺された無辜の人々のためだけでなく
かつて希望をもって　まともで輝いていた我々が
緩慢な死に近づき
虚しい約束の針でしぼんでしまった今
部分的に我々のために
埋葬の塚を一層また一層と重ねながら
我々をすり潰している

臆病な時代の戦争

ベトナムから学んだ教訓

嘘からはじめよう　勇敢な者ほど良い
図表は役にたつ

徴兵をやめなさい　貧しい者たちに
除隊の後の教育を約束しなさい

民衆に戦争は民主主義を救う　あるいは
広めるだろうといいなさい

Claim victory or argue it is right around the corner.

Don't do body counts. Hide the body bags.

Use fewer troops, and bomb from high altitudes.

Don't allow photos of the returning coffins.

Keep lying.

New Rules

Fight preventive wars at a time of our choosing.

International law is irrelevant.

You are either with us or with the enemy.

Embed the press.

Detain prisoners indefinitely, without rights.

Authorize torture, then blame the soldiers
who administer it.

If in doubt, swagger.

勝利を言い張りなさい　さもなければ　勝利は
もうすぐそこだと主張しなさい

死体の勘定をするな　死体の袋をかくしなさい

出来るだけ部隊をつかわずに　高い所から爆撃しなさい

もどってゆく棺の写真をとるのは禁止しなさい

嘘をつきつづけなさい

新しい規則

時を選んで先制攻撃をせよ

国際法など無関係

味方か敵かのどちらかだ

報道陣をはめ込め

権利をあたえずに　囚人たちを無期限に拘留しなさい

拷問を正当化せよ　そしてそれを行った
兵隊たちを非難せよ

迷っているなら　ふんぞりかえって歩け

Soldiers Fall

War spreads
its sad red wings.

Soldiers fall
like white flowers
on a winter field.

They sink
in burning snow.

兵士たちは倒れる

戦争は拡大した
その悲しい赤い翼

兵士たちは倒れる
冬野に
白い花のように

彼らは沈む
燃えている雪のなかに

Oh, War

Oh, war, let us count the ways we'll use you.
To profit, to add excitement to the dullness of our lives,
to unite our country, to make our young men dashing,
to profit, to give new meaning to our lives, to prove
ourselves on fields of battle, to stimulate our poets,
to rally round our flag, to bring forth the eloquence
of our leaders, to defeat the barbarians, to add medals
to our uniforms, to profit, to put us to the test of battle,
to defend what we love most, to conquer, to save
our leaders from the compromise of peace, to expand
our territory, to use our weapons and create new ones,
to profit, to heighten love by loss, to sacrifice, to add
glory to our history, to love more deeply, to protect
our oil supply, to immortalize ourselves, to profit.

おお　戦争よ

おお　戦争よ　お前を利用する方法を数えてみよう
儲けること　我々の退屈な人生に刺激を増すこと
国を一体化すること　若者たちを突進させること
儲けること　我々の人生に新しい意味を与えること
戦場で自分自身を試すこと　詩人たちを刺激すること
国旗のもとにはせ参ずること　指導者たちの雄弁を
実らせること　野蛮人たちを打ち負かすこと　制服に
勲章を増やすこと　儲けること　戦争を試してみること
我々が最も愛するものを守ること　征服すること
平和への妥協から指導者たちを救うこと　領土を
増やすこと　武器を使用し新兵器を造りだすこと
儲けること　喪失をとおして愛を高揚させること　犠牲になること
我々の歴史に栄光を与えること　もっと深く愛すること　我々の
石油の供給を守ること　自分たちを不朽にすること　儲けること

IV

EINSTEIN'S REGRET

アインシュタインの悔い

Einstein's Regret

Einstein's regret ran deep
Like the pools of sorrow
That were his eyes.

His mind could see things
That others could not,
The bending of light,

The slowing of time,
Relationships of trains passing
In the night, and power,

Dormant and asleep,
That could be awakened,
But who would dare?

He saw patterns
In snowflakes and stars,
Unimaginable simplicity.

When the shadow of Hitler
Spread across Europe
What was Einstein to do?

アインシュタインの悔い

アインシュタインの悔いは深くなった
彼の目にある
悲しみの湛えのように

彼の頭脳は他者が
見ることのできない物事を見通せた
光の屈折

時間の遅れ
夜間走っている列車の
関係性と力

休眠中であろうと就寝中であろうと
目覚めることはできるが
誰があえてそうしようとしたか

彼は　雪片と星の
パターンを見出した
想像もできない単純さ

ヒットラーの影が
ヨーロッパに蔓延した時
アインシュタインは何をしたのか？

His regret ran deep, deeper
Than the pools of sorrow
That were his eyes.

A Short History Lesson: 1945

August 6th:
Dropped atomic bomb
On civilians
At Hiroshima.

August 8th:
Agreed to hold
War crimes trials
For Nazis.

August 9th:
Dropped atomic bomb
On civilians
At Nagasaki.

彼の悔いは深くなった
彼の目の悲しみの湛えよりも
もっと　深くなった

短い歴史のレッスン：1945年

八月六日
原子爆弾を投下した
ヒロシマの
市民の上に

八月八日
ナチにたいする
戦争犯罪裁判を
行う決議をした

八月九日
原子爆弾を投下した
ナガサキの
市民の上に

August Mornings

Hiroshima

Clear summer morning—
The steel-hearted bomb
Just a speck in the sky

Nagasaki

The bomb shatters
The humid summer silence—
Severs the heads of stone saints

八月の朝

ヒロシマ

夏の快晴の朝――
スチール製の心をもった爆弾は
大空の小さな一点にすぎなかった

ナガサキ

爆弾は打ち砕いた
湿度の高い夏の静寂を――
石造の聖人たちの頭を断ち割った

Hiroshima

The city wears a cloak of grief
in the air and on the streets,

in the way people move and speak,
in the lights and sounds of the city.

What else must we know about the future
than this: flames and ashes.

It is not enough that flowers have grown
in Hiroshima when so many people have died.

The heat has melted time. Everything is charred.
Even the sunlight is filtered by sadness.

ヒロシマ

この街は悲しみの外套をまとっている
大気にそして街路に

人々が動きそして話す様子に
この街の光や音に

これ以外に何を未来について
知らねばならないだろう──炎と灰

ヒロシマに花が育っていることで充分とすることはできない
そんなにも多くの人々が死んでいるのだから

あの熱は時間を溶解した　すべてのものは黒焦げになった
日の光さえ悲しみで濾過されている

Forgive Me, Mother
for Shoji Sawada

After the bomb, the young boy
awakened beneath the rubble of his room.

He could hear his mother's cries,
still trapped within the fallen house.

He struggled to free her, but he lacked
the strength.

A fire raged toward them. Many people
hurried past.

Frightened and dazed, they would not stop
to help him free his mother.

He could hear her voice from the rubble.
The voice was soft but firm.

"You must run and save yourself,"
she told him. "You must go."

"Forgive me," he said, bowing,
"Forgive me, Mother."

He did as his mother wished.
That was long ago, in 1945.

The boy has long been a man, a good man.
Yet he still runs from those flames.

お母さん　許して
沢田昭二のために

爆撃の後　幼い少年は
自分の部屋の瓦礫の下で気がついた

彼は倒れた家の中にまだ閉じこめられている
母の叫び声を聞いた

彼は母を逃がそうともがいた
しかし　力が足りなかった

火が迫ってきた
多くの人々が急いで通りすぎた

驚愕し茫然とした人々は　彼の母を逃がす
助けをするために立ち止ってはくれなかった

彼は瓦礫のなかから母の声を聞いた
その声はやさしかったがしっかりとしていた

「お前は逃げ　自分を守りなさい」
彼女は「いかなければだめ」と言った

「お母さん　許して」頭をさげて彼は言った
「私を許して　お母さん」

彼は母親の望んだようにした
それは昔のこと 1945 年のことだ

少年はもうずいぶん前に大人になった　立派な大人に
けれど彼は今もなお　あの炎から逃げている

Among the Ashes

Among the ashes
of Hiroshima
were crisply charred bodies.

In one of the charred bodies
a daughter recognized
the gold tooth of her mother.

As the girl reached out
to touch the burnt body
her mother crumbled to ashes.

Her mother, so vivid
in the girl's memory, sifted
through her hands, floated away.

灰のなかで

ヒロシマの
灰のなかで
パリパリに焼け焦げた死体があった

それら黒焦げの死体のなかで
娘は母の金歯を
見付けた

少女が　その焼死体に触れようと
手を伸ばした時
母は崩れて灰になった

少女の記憶のなかで
そんなに鮮明だった母は　彼女の手から
ふるいおとされて　漂い去ってしまった

Nagasaki

When the bomb fell, fierce winds blew
and the wooden houses went up in flame.
Many people died, leaving behind dark shadows,
unfinished lives.

Now, seven decades later, rain falls
on the black obelisk that marks the epicenter
of the detonation.

Since that day long ago, how little
we have learned, how comfortable we've grown
with the bomb.

ナガサキ

爆弾が落ちた時　すさまじい爆風が吹き
木造の家々は炎に包まれた
多くの人々が死んだ　背後に黒い影を
未完の命を残して

七十年後の現在
爆心地を示す黒いオベリスクに
雨が降る

遠い昔のあの日から　我々が
学んだことの何と少ないことか
何とぬくぬくと爆弾とともにすごしてきたことか

Echoes in the Sky

"Today the bells of Nagasaki echo in the sky..."
—— Mayor Iccho Itoh, Nagasaki

The clouds parted and made space for devastation.
The city, so welcoming, deserved far better.

Before anyone expected, the flowers returned.
Memories are painful, sometimes unbearable.

The words of apology never came. The survivors
grow old and feeble. Generations pass.

The air above the sea is thick with sorrow.
The bells echo in the sky's embrace.

空のこだま

　　「今日　長崎の鐘は空に鳴る」
　　　　　──伊藤一長　長崎市長

雲は分かれ　灰燼に帰すためのスペースを作った
その街は　そのように歓迎して　もっといいことに値した

誰もが期待する以前に　花はもどってきた
記憶は痛ましく　時には耐え難かった

謝罪の言葉など全くなかった　生存者たちは
年老い　弱っていった　何世代もの人たちが死んだ

海の上の空気は悲しみで覆われている
空に抱かれて鐘は鳴る

Eisenhower's View

"It wasn't necessary to hit them with that awful thing"
———— General Dwight D. Eisenhower

We hit them with it, first
at Hiroshima and then at Nagasaki—
the old one-two punch.

The bombings were tests really, to see
what those "awful things" would do.

First, of a gun-type uranium bomb, and then
of a plutonium implosion bomb.

Both proved highly effective
in the art of obliterating cities.

It wasn't necessary.

アイゼンハワーの見解

「彼らをそんな恐るべきもので攻撃する必要はなかった」
　　　　　　　——ドワイト・D・アイゼンハワー将軍

　我々は彼らをそれで攻撃した　最初は
　ヒロシマ　それから　ナガサキ——
　昔ながらのワン・ツウー・パンチだ

　爆撃は　本当はテストだった　それらの
　「恐るべきもの」がどの程度やるかを見るためだった

　最初は銃砲タイプのウラニウム爆弾　それから
　プルトニウムの内破爆弾

　両方とも非常に有効なことは証明された
　都市を抹消する技術として

　それは必要でなかった

Where Did the Victims Go?

Where else would the victims go but first
into the air, then into the water, then into the grasses,
and eventually into our food?

I speak of the victims incinerated at Hiroshima
and Nagasaki, those too close to the center
who were caught in the heat and fire
of our new power.

I speak of the victims burned away
to their elemental particles, to atoms,
similar to other atoms, let loose into the atmosphere
to drift and fall without volition.

What does this mean?
It means that we breathe our victims,
that we drink them and eat them, without tasting
the bitterness, in our daily meals.

It means there is no way to live without ourselves
becoming, in subtle and powerful ways,
those we have destroyed.

犠牲者たちはどこへいったのか？

犠牲者たちは　最初は空気　それから
水の中　それから草の中　そして最後は
我々の食物のなかにはいらずに　どこへゆけたのだろう？

私はヒロシマ　そしてナガサキで焼き殺された
犠牲者たちについて話している　爆心地に非常に近く
我々の新しいエネルギーの熱と炎に
捕らえられた人々のことだ

私は元素の粒子
他の類似した原子と同様な原子にまで焼かれ
自分の意志でなく　大気のなかに放たれ　漂い　落下した
犠牲者たちについて話している

それは何を意味しているか？
それは我々が犠牲者たちを　呼吸し
飲み　我々の日々の食事に
彼らの痛苦を味わうことなく　彼ら食べているのだ

それは　我々自身　微妙なものであろうと強大なものであろうと
自分たちが破壊したものになろうとするよりほか
生きる道はないことを意味している

On Becoming Death

"Now I am become death, the destroyer of worlds."
—Bhagavad Gita

When Oppenheimer thought, "Now *I am* become death," did he mean, "Now *we have* become death"? Was Oppenheimer thinking about himself or all of us?

That August of '45 Truman and his military boys *destroyed* a few worlds. They never understood that among the worlds they destroyed was their own.

From Alamogordo to Hiroshima took exactly three weeks. On August 6th, Oppenheimer again became death. So did Groves, Stimson and Byrnes So did Truman. So did a seventy thousand that day in Hiroshima. And so did America.

"This is the greatest thing in history," Truman said. He didn't think *he'd* become death *that* day. We Americans know how to win. Truman was a winner, a *destroyer of worlds*. Three days later, Truman and his military boys did it again at Nagasaki.

Sometime later, Oppenheimer visited Truman. "I have blood on my hands," Oppenheimer said. Truman didn't like those words.

死神になること

「今や我は世界の破壊者　死神になった」
　　　　　　──バガヴァッド・ギーター[*1]（神の詩）

オッペンハイマー[*2]が「*私は　今や死神になった*」と考えた時
彼は「*我々は　今や死神になった*」ということを意味していたのだろうか？
オッペンハイマーは彼自身のことを考えていたのか
それとも我々全体のことを考えていたのか

45年8月トルーマンと若手の軍人たちは　二、三の世界を　*破壊した*
彼らは世界の中で自分たち自身の世界を
破壊したことを決して理解していなかった

アラモゴルド[*3]からヒロシマまで正確には三週間かかった　八月六日
オッペンハイマーは再び死神になった　グローブズ[*4]も　スティムソン[*5]も
そしてバインズ[*6]も死神になった　トルーマンもそうだった
その日ヒロシマで七万人が死んだ　そしてアメリカも死神になった

「これは歴史的に偉大なことだ」とトルーマンは言った　彼は　その日　彼が
死神になったと思わなかった　我々アメリカ人はどうしたら勝てるか知っている
トルーマンは勝者であった　*世界の破壊者*　であった　三日後
トルーマンと若手の軍人たちは　それをナガサキでふたたび行なった

しばらくしてオッペンハイマーはトルーマンを訪ねた
「私の手は血塗られている」とオッペンハイマーは言った
トルーマンはそうした言葉を好まなかった

Blood? What blood? When Oppenheimer left, Truman said, "Don't ever let him in here again."

The Deep Bow of a *Hibakusha*
for Miyoko Matsubara

She bowed deeply. She bowed deeper than the oceans. She bowed from the top of Mt. Fuji to the bottom of the ocean. She bowed so deeply and so often that the winds blew hard.

The winds blew her whispered apologies and prayers across all the continents. But the winds whistled too loudly, and made it impossible to hear her apologies and prayers. The winds made the oceans crazy. The water in the oceans rose up in a wild molecular dance. The oceans threw themselves against the continents. The people were frightened. They ran screaming from the shores. They feared the white water and the whistling wind. They huddled together in dark places. They strained to hear the words in the wind.

In some places there were some people who thought they heard an apology. In other places there were people who thought they heard a prayer.

She bowed deeply. She bowed more deeply than anyone should bow.

血？　何の血が？　オッペンハイマーが去った時　トルーマンは言った
「彼を二度とここに入れるな」

＊１　サンスクリット語で書かれたヒンズーの経典　　＊４　マンハッタン計画のアメリカ合衆国将軍
＊２　最初の核兵器マンハッタン計画の科学者　　　　＊５　トルーマンの国防長官
＊３　アメリカ合衆国ニューメキシコ州の都市。　　　＊６　トルーマンの国防長官
　　　主要な軍事基地

被爆者の最敬礼
松原美代子さんのために

彼女は最敬礼をした　彼女は海よりも深く礼をした　彼女は
富士山の山頂から大洋の底に向かって礼をした　彼女は最敬礼を
非常に度々したので　風が激しく吹いた

風は彼女の謝罪と祈りのつぶやきをすべての大陸へと運んでいった
けれども風はあまりに強く吹いたので彼女の謝罪と祈りは聞こえなかった
風は海の気を狂わせた　海水は荒々しい分子のダンスをして盛り上がった
大洋は大陸に向かって押し寄せた　人々は驚愕した
彼らは叫びながら海岸から逃げた
彼らは白い波と唸りをあげる風を恐れた
彼らは暗い場所に身を寄せ合った
彼らは精一杯風のなかの言葉を聞こうとした

ある場所で　謝罪を聞いたと思う人々がいた
他の場所では
祈りを聞いたと思う人たちがいた

彼女は最敬礼をした　彼女はほかの誰かがすべきと思うよりも
　　　もっと深く礼をした

A Grandmother's Story

The grandmother looked into the eyes
of her granddaughter, recalling the day
the bomb dropped on Hiroshima. The sky
was bluest blue, she said. And when
the sky exploded the wind knocked me
off my feet. All around me there were screams
that still echo in my ears, children calling
for their mothers. The wounded walked past us
with vacant stares, their skin hanging
like ribbons from their bodies. Hiroshima
became a city of death. We lost all will to live
until new shoots of grass appeared.

With them, the darkness melted
into small green blades of hope.

あるおばあさんの物語

おばあさんは　ヒロシマに原爆が
落ちた日を回想しながら
孫娘の目をみつめた　空は
この上もなく青かった　と彼女は言った
空で爆発があった時　風は私を
なぎ倒した　周りじゅう今でも耳に
残っている叫び声　子供たちが
母親をよんでいる声がおこった
負傷者たちは虚ろな目をして通り過ぎた
彼らの皮膚は体からリボンのように
垂れ下がっていた　ヒロシマは
死の街になった　私たちは草の新芽が
現れるまで生きるという意志を失くした

草とともに　暗闇は
希望の小さな緑の葉になった

God Responded with Tears

The plane flew over Hiroshima and dropped the bomb
after the all clear warning had sounded.

The bomb dropped far slower than the speed of light.
It dropped at the speed of bombs.

From the ground it was a tiny silver speck
that separated from the silver plane.

After 43 seconds, the slow falling bomb exploded
into mass at the speed of light squared.

Einstein called it energy. Everything lit up.
For a split-second people could see their own bones.

The pilot always believed he had done the right thing.
The President, too, never wavered from his belief.

He thanked God for the bomb. Others did, too.
God responded with tears that fell far slower

than the speed of bombs.
They still have not reached Earth.

神は涙をもって応えた

飛行機はヒロシマ上空を飛んだ　そして
警報解除が鳴り渡った後　原爆を投下した

原爆は光の速度よりもゆっくりと落下していった
爆弾の速度で落ちていった

地上から見ると　それは銀色の飛行機から
切り離された小さな銀色の斑点であった

四十三秒後　ゆっくりと降下した爆弾は
光速の弐乗でいくつにも爆発した

アインシュタインはそれをエネルギーと呼んだ　すべてが燃え上がった
あっという間に　自分達の骨が見えた

パイロットは常に自分は正しいことをしたと信じていた
大統領もまた自分の信念を決してゆるがせなかった

彼は原爆について神に感謝した　他の者たちも同様だった
神は爆弾の速度よりも

はるかにゆっくりと落ちる涙で応えた
その涙はまだ地表にはとどいていない

The Four Seasons of Hiroshima

Summer
a quiet morning
suddenly the sun explodes

Autumn
the people wander
through the ash

Winter
without the sun
the cold penetrates

Spring
the grasses return
and the plum blossoms

ヒロシマの四季

夏
静かな朝
突然　太陽が爆発した

秋
人々は灰の中を
さまよった

冬
太陽はなく
寒さが刺し貫いた

春
草はまた生え
梅の花が咲いた

Testing Nuclear Weapons in the Marshall Islands

The islands were alive
with the red-orange fire of sunset
splashed across a billowy sky.
The islanders lived simple lives
close to the edge of the ocean planet
reaching out to infinity.

The days were bright and the nights
calm in this happy archipelago
until the colonizers came: the Spanish,
Germans, Japanese and then, worst of all,
the United States.

The U.S. came as trustee
bearing its new bombs, eager to test them
in this beautiful barefoot Eden.
The islanders were trusting,
even when the bombs began exploding
and the white ash fell like snow.

The children played
in the ash as it floated down on them,
covering them in poison.

The rest is a tale of loss
and suffering by the islanders, of madness
by the people of the bomb.

マーシャル群島での核兵器実験

島は波のような雲に
赤とオレンジ色の夕日の炎が
まだらに散って生き生きとしていた
島人たちは無限にまでとどくような
海惑星の端近くに住み
シンプルな生活を送っていた

幸せな列島の昼は明るく
夜は静かだった
植民地化されるまでは——
スペイン人　ドイツ人　日本人それから
最悪のアメリカ合衆国がやってきた

アメリカは新爆弾をもって　その受託人として
やってきた　この美しいはだしのエデンで
熱心にその実験をしようとしていた
島人たちは信頼していた
原爆が破裂し　雪のように
白い灰が降った時でさえも

子供たちは　灰が彼らの上に舞い降り
毒で彼らを覆っても
灰の中で遊んでいた

その後は島人たちの喪失と
苦悩の物語であり　原爆人間の
狂気の物語である

What Shall We Call the Bomb Dropped on Hiroshima?

Shall we call it
Flash of White Light Maker or
Mushroom Cloud in Sky Maker?

Shall we call it
Terminator of War Bomb or
Incinerator of People Weapon?

Shall we call it
Secret Victory Weapon or
Dark Shadow Revealing Bomb?

Shall we call it
Rescuer of Young Soldiers Weapon or
Creator of Orphans Bomb?

Shall we call it
The Beginning of the End or
The End of the Beginning?

ヒロシマに落ちた爆弾をなんと呼ぶべきか？

我々はそれを
白光の創造者の閃光と呼ぶべきか
それとも空の創造者のキノコ雲と呼ぶべきだろうか？

我々はそれを
究極の戦闘用爆弾と呼ぶべきか
あるいは人類の武器の焼却炉と呼ぶべきだろうか？

我々はそれを
勝利をもたらす秘密兵器と呼ぶべきか
あるいは暗い影を出現させる爆弾と呼ぶべきだろうか？

我々はそれを
若い兵士救済爆弾と呼ぶべきか
孤児製造爆弾と呼ぶべきだろうか？

我々はそれを
終末のはじまりと呼ぶべきか
あるいははじまりの終末と呼ぶべきだろうか？

When the Bomb Became Our God

When the bomb became our god
We loved it far too much,
Worshipping no other gods before it.

We thought ourselves great
And powerful, creators of worlds.

We turned toward infinity,
Giving the bomb our very souls.

We looked to it for comfort,
To its smooth metallic grace.

When the bomb became our god
We lived in a constant state of war
That we called *peace*.

原爆が神になった日

原爆が我々の神になった時
我々はそれをあまりにも愛し
その前で他の神を拝むことを止めた

我々は自分たちを偉大だ
強大だ　世界の創造者だなどと考えた

我々は永遠の方を向き
その爆弾に我々の魂さえ与えた

我々はそれに快さを見ようとした
その滑らかで金属的な優美さに

原爆が我々の神になった時
我々が　*平和*　と呼んでいる
恒常的な戦争状態に生きているのだ

Twelve Possible Names for World War III

The Great Fire War

The Long Afternoon War

The End of Civilization War

The Unwanted War

The Failure of Deterrence War

The Ice Age Trigger War

The No Heroes War

The Mutant Creation War

The Dark Skies War

The Unending Fall-Out War

The Green Glow of Defeat War

The War of No Winners

十二の第三次世界大戦名予測

大火災戦

長い午後戦争

文明終末戦

望まれなかった戦い

抑止力失敗の戦争

氷河期きっかけの戦争

英雄なき戦争

突然変異創造戦争

暗黒の空戦争

終わりなき放射性降下物戦争

敗北の緑の光戦争

勝者なき戦争

The Merry-Go-Round

The end could begin with a missile launched by accident.
And then the response would be deliberate, as would be
the counter-response, and on and on until we were all
gone.

Or, it could be deliberate from the outset, an act
of madness by a suicidal leader, setting the end in motion.

First, the blasts and mushroom clouds. Then the fires
and burning cities and the winds driving the fires, turning
humans into projectiles, and all of it mixed with deadly
radiation. Finally, for the last act, the soot from destroyed
cities rising into the upper stratosphere, blocking the sunlight
and the temperatures falling into a frozen Ice Age, followed
by mass starvation.

If any humans were left to name it, they might call it
"Global Hiroshima," but none would be left.
It would be ugly for a while, eerily still and silent
for some stretch of time, but no one would be there
to observe. Still, the Earth would go on rotating
around the sun and the universe would go on expanding.

Only we humans would be off the not-so-merry-go-round.

メリーゴーランド

終末は事故で発射したミサイルで始まり
その報復は入念であろう
反撃がそうであるように　どんどんエスカレートして
ついには誰もいなくなる

さもなければ　最初から入念であり得る
自爆指導者の狂気の行動は　死を実行に移したものだ

最初に　爆風とキノコ雲　それから火災と炎上する街
火をあおる風　人間を発射物に変え
それらすべては致命的な放射能に混ぜ合わされる
最後に　最後の動きとして
破壊された都市から成層圏上部にまで立ち昇る煤は
太陽光をさえぎり　気温は氷河期まで下がり
次に大規模な餓死がおこる

もし人類の誰かが残り　それを名づけるとすれば
「世界規模のヒロシマ」と言っていいだろうが　誰も残れないだろう
暫くは醜い　ぬるぬるした静寂と沈黙の　いくらかの時間の延長
しかし　誰もそれを観察する者はいないだろう
地球はなおも太陽の周りを自転しつづけ
宇宙は膨張しつづけるであろう

我々人類だけが　楽しくもないそんなメリーゴーランドから降りる
　のであろう

A Butterfly Blinked

A butterfly blinked
and it is no longer the Stone Age
or even the Iron Age.

Leaving a white trail
a silver airplane cut through the sky
and disappeared.

One nuclear bomb
destroyed Hiroshima, shadows
etched in concrete.

Without thinking,
they dropped another nuclear bomb
on Madame Butterfly's city.

Now, the flame is eternal,
the one kept burning at Koyasan Temple
surrounded by prayers.

蝶は目をぱちぱちさせた

蝶は目をぱちぱちさせた
もはや石器時代でも
鉄器時代でさえもなかった

白い飛行機雲を残して
銀色の飛行機は空を切って飛び
消え去った

一つの核爆弾は
ヒロシマを破壊し　影は
コンクリートに刻まれた

考えもせずに
彼らはもう一つの核爆弾を
マダム・バタフライの街に落とした

今や　炎は永遠になった
祈る人々に囲まれて
一つは高野山寺院で燃えている

V

A CONSPIRACY OF DECENCY

礼儀正しき共謀

A Conspiracy of Decency

We will conspire to keep this blue dot floating and alive,
to keep the soldiers from gunning down the children,

to make the water clean and clear and plentiful,
to put food on everybody's table and hope in their hearts.

We will conspire to find new ways to say People matter.
This conspiracy will be bold.

Everyone will dance at wholly inappropriate times.
They will burst out singing non-patriotic songs.

And the not-so-secret password will be *Peace*.

礼儀正しき共謀

我々はこの青い惑星を浮かべ生存させておける
兵士たちが子供たちを撃ち殺すのを止めさせることができる

水を清潔にして澄んで十分あるようにすることができる
食べ物を皆のテーブルにのせ彼らの心に希望をもたせることができる

我々は人民の問題という新しい方法を見つけるためにともに働くことができるだろう
この共謀は際立つだろう

どの人も全く不適当な時間にダンスをするだろう
彼らは突然愛国的でない歌を歌いだすだろう

そしてそんなに秘密でないパスワードは 平和 であろう

Today Is Not a Good Day for War

Today is not a good day for war,
Not when the sun is shining,
And leaves are trembling in the breeze.

Today is not a good day for bombs to fall,
Not when clouds hang on the horizon
And drift above the sea.

Today is not a good day for young men to die,
Not when they have so many dreams
And so much still to do.

Today is not a good day to send missiles flying,
Not when the fog rolls in
And the rain is falling hard.

Today is not a good day for launching attacks,
Not when families gather
And hold on to one another.

Today is not a good day for collateral damage,
Not when children are restless
Daydreaming of frogs and creeks.

今日は戦争をするのにいい日ではない

今日は戦争をするのにいい日ではない
太陽が輝き
木の葉が微風にそよいでいるのだから　ノー

今日は爆弾を投下するのにいい日ではない
水平線に雲が垂れ込め
海上に漂っているのだから　ノー

今日は若者が命を落とすのにいい日ではない
彼等はたくさんの夢をもち
まだやりたいことが沢山あるのだから　ノー

今日はミサイルを発射するのにいい日ではない
霧が渦巻き
雨が激しく降っているのだから　ノー

今日は攻撃をしかけるのにいい日ではない
家族たちが集まって
互いに支えあっているのだから　ノー

今日は戦闘地域外に損害を与えるのにいい日ではない
子供達はそわそわと
蛙や小川の夢を白昼みているのだから　ノー

Today is not a good day for war,
Not when birds are soaring,
Filling the sky with grace.

No matter what they tell us about *the other*,
Nor how bold their patriotic calls,
Today is not a good day for war.

今日は戦争をするのにいい日ではない
鳥たちが飛翔し
空を恩寵で満たしているのだから　ノー

彼等がいかに　そうでない　と言おうとも
愛国的な叫びがいかに勇ましくとも
今日は戦争をするのにいい日ではない

Worse Than the War

Worse than the war, the endless, senseless war,
Worse than the lies leading to the war,

Worse than the countless deaths and injuries,
Worse than hiding the coffins and not attending funerals,

Worse than the flouting of international law,
Worse than the torture at Abu Ghraib prison,

Worse than the corruption of young soldiers,
Worse than undermining our collective sense of decency,

Worse than the arrogance, smugness and swagger,
Worse than our loss of credibility in the world,
Worse than the loss of our liberties,

Worse than learning nothing from the past,
Worse than destroying the future,
Worse than the incredible stupidity of it all,

Worse than all of these,
As if they were not enough for one war or country or lifetime,
Is the silence, the resounding silence of good Americans.

戦争より悪い

戦争よりも悪い　終わりのない　愚かな戦
戦争へ導く嘘よりも悪い

数えきれない死者たちや負傷者たちよりも悪い
棺を隠したり葬儀に参列しないことよりも悪い

国際法に従わないよりも悪い
アブ・グラブ牢獄の拷問よりも悪い

若い兵士たちの堕落よりも悪い
体裁についての集合意識をひそかに傷つけるよりも悪い

傲慢　独りよがり　威張り散らすことよりも悪い
世間での信用を失うことよりも悪い
自由の喪失よりも悪い

過去から何も学ばないことよりも悪い
未来を破壊するよりも悪い
それらすべての信じられないような愚かさよりも悪い

これら全部よりも悪いのは
あたかも戦争や国家や人生といったものに値しないかのような
善良なアメリカ人たちの沈黙　徹底的な沈黙である

Standing with Pablo

"I have a higher duty to my conscience..."
———Pablo Paredes

Like the three tenors, like three pillars,
there are three Pablos for peace:
Picasso, Neruda and Paredes.

The first painted *Guernica*, the second
wrote poems as an act of peace.
The third refuses to fight in Iraq.

There is talk about *the conscience of mankind*.
But there is no such thing, only
the conscience of each individual.

Pablo Picasso painted the horrors of war.
Pablo Neruda wrote poems of love and decency.
Pablo Paredes refused to kill or be killed.

The three Pablos are comrades *against* arms.
They stand together for human dignity.
Should we not stand with them?

パブロとともに立つ

　「*私は私の良心にたいして高度の義務をもつ*」
　　　　　　　　——パブロ　パレデ

三人のテノール歌手のように　三本の柱のように
平和のためにつくした三人のパブロがいる
ピカソ　ネルダ　パレデである

最初の人は *ゲルニカ* を画いた
次の人は平和活動としての詩を書いた
三人目の人はイラクで戦うのを拒否した

人間としての良心 についての議論はある
しかし　個人の良心についてだけの
議論というものはない

パブロ・ピカソは戦争の恐怖を描いた
パブロ・ネルダは愛と礼儀の詩を書いた
パブロ・パレデは殺すこと　或いは殺されることを拒否した

三人のパブロは武器に *反対する* 仲間だった
彼らは共に人間の尊厳について立ち上がった
我々は彼らと共に立つべきではないのか？

I Refuse
for Camilo Mejia

I refuse to be used as a tool
of war.

I refuse to kill on order.

I refuse to give my life for a lie.

I refuse to be indoctrinated
or subordinated.

I refuse to allow the military to define
all I can be.

I refuse to abdicate my responsibilities
as a citizen of the world.

I refuse to deny the human rights
of any person.

I refuse to suspend my conscience.

I refuse to give up my humanity.

I refuse to be silenced.

Do you hear me?

私は拒否する
カミロ・メジア*のために

私は戦争の道具として使われるのを
拒否する

私は命令で殺すことを拒否する

私は虚偽のために私の命をさしだすのを拒否する

私は教化されることも
従わされることも拒否する

私は軍隊が　私が成れるすべて　を決める
ことも拒否する

私は世界の市民としての私の責任を放棄するのを
拒否する

私はすべての人の人権を否定することを
拒否する

私は私の良心を一時休止にするのを拒否する

私は自分の人間性を断念することを拒否する

私は沈黙させられるのを拒否する

私の言っていること聞こえるか？

＊イラクのアメリカ軍にいた若いニカラグアの兵士

The Doves Flew High

What if they gave a war and no one came?

The president stood before Congress
and, as presidents do, called for war.

The members of Congress, oblivious
to their duties, jumped to their feet cheering.

When he was ready, the president gave the order
for war in his most commanding voice.

But no soldiers were there to receive it—
no general, no colonel, no captain,
no sergeant, no private, no soldier at all.

The young men and women stayed in school
or at their work, voting with their bodies
against war.

The Congress was somber and sober.
Without soldiers, they matured.

The president, devoid of options, chose peace.
And the doves flew high.

鳩は高く飛んだ

戦争になっても誰も来なかったらどうなるのか？

大統領は議会の前に立ち
大統領として戦争を宣言した

議員たちは義務を忘れて
立ち上がって歓声をあげた

準備ができた時　大統領は
最も威圧的な声で開戦の命令をだした

しかし　それを受ける兵士は誰もいなかった
将官も　佐官も　尉官も
下士官も　民間人も　兵士は誰もいなかった

若者も女性たちも学校や仕事場にいた
体を張って戦争反対の投票をした

議会は沈鬱になり正気になっていった
兵士なしで　彼らは大人になった

大統領は　選択の余地が無くなって　平和を選んだ
そして鳩は高く飛んだ

Wake Up!

The alarm is sounding.
Can you hear it?

Can you hear the bells
of Nagasaki
ringing out for peace?

Can you feel the heartbeat
of Hiroshima
pulsing out for life?

The survivors of Hiroshima
and Nagasaki
are growing older.

Their message is clear:
Never again!

Wake up!
Now, before the feathered arrow
is placed into the bow.

Now, before the string
of the bow is pulled taut,
the arrow poised for flight.

目を覚ませ！

警報は鳴っている
聞こえますか？

ナガサキの鐘が
平和を求めて鳴っているのが
聞こえますか？

ヒロシマの鼓動を
感じることができますか？
命を求めて脈うっている鼓動を

ヒロシマ　ナガサキの
生存者は
だんだん年をとってゆく

彼らのメッセージは明確である
決して　再び！

目を覚ませ！
今、羽のある矢が
弓につがえられる前に

今　弓の弦が
ピンと張られる前に
矢は飛ぶ前の均衡をたもっている

Now, before the arrow is let loose,
before it flies across oceans
and continents.

Now, before we are engulfed in flames,
while there is still time, while we still can,
Wake up!

The One-Hearted

The one-hearted walk a lonely trail.
They hold the dream of peace between
the moon's eclipse and the rising sun.

They set down their weapons, carrying
instead the spirits of their ancestors,
a collection of smooth stones.

At night, they make fires, and watch
the smoke rise into the starlit sky.

They are warriors of hope, navigating
oceans and crossing continents.

Their message is simple: Now
is the time for peace. It always has been.

今　矢が放たれる前に
海を越え
大陸を越えて飛んでゆく前に

今　我々が炎に包まれる前に
まだ時間があるうちに　我々がまだできるうちに
目を覚ませ！

ひたむきな人々

ひたむきな心をもった人々は連れのいない道を歩く
彼らは月蝕と日の出の間に
平和という夢をかかげている

彼らは武器を置いた　代わりに
祖先の魂の
すべすべした石のコレクションを運んだ

夜には　彼らは火をおこした　そして煙が
星の輝く空に昇ってゆくのを見つめた

彼らは希望の戦士だった
海を航海し大陸を横断した

彼らのメッセージは明快であった：今は
平和の時　いつも常にそうであった

Great Truth Has Great Silence

*"The small truth has words that are clear;
the great truth has great silence."*
—Rabindranath Tagore

When light races across the universe
it runs on silent feet.

While night stretches its dark wings across
the sky, the moon is enveloped in silence.

As trees grow toward the sky and dance
in the wind, their roots sink silently.

In the deepest reaches of the forest, where
no birds call, there is silence.

When fine minds commune across time
and space, thoughts travel silently.

Where love is strong, there is no need
for words.

Within the awful shattering chaos of war,
lives a still and silent seed of peace.

偉大な真実は偉大な沈黙

「小さな真実は明快な言葉をもっている；
　大きな真実は偉大な沈黙をもっている」
　　　　　　　　——ラビンドラナ　タゴール

光が宇宙を横切る時
それは無音の足音でゆく

夜がその暗い翼を空に広げる時
月は沈黙に包まれている

木々が空に向かって成長し風の中で
踊る時　その根はしずかに沈んでゆく

森の一番深いところでは　鳥は鳴かず
沈黙がある

すばらしい精神が時空を越えて親しく
交わる時　思想はしずかに旅をする

愛が強い時　言葉は
いらない

戦争でひどく粉砕された混迷のうちに
静かで無言の平和の種子は生きる

VI

FIFTY-ONE REASONS FOR HOPE

希望のための五十一の理由

Fifty-one Reasons for Hope

1. Each new dawn.
2. The miracle of birth.
3. Our capacity to love.
4. The courage of nonviolence.
5. Gandhi, King and Mandela.
6. The night sky.
7. Spring.
8. Flowers and bees.
9. The arc of justice.
10. Whistleblowers.
11. Butterflies.
12. The full moon.
13. Teachers.
14. Simple wisdom.
15. Dogs and cats.
16. Friendship.
17. Our ability to reflect.
18. Our capacity for joy.
19. The Dalai Lama, Desmond Tutu and Oscar Romero.
20. The gift of conscience.
21. Human rights and responsibilities.
22. Our capacity to nurture.
23. The ascendancy of women.
24. Innocence.
25. Our capacity to change.

希望のための五十一の理由

1. それぞれの新たな夜明け
2. 誕生という奇蹟
3. 愛するという能力
4. 非暴力の勇気
5. ガンジー　キング　マンデラ
6. 夜空
7. 春
8. 花と蜜蜂たち
9. 正義のアーチ
10. 口笛を吹く人たち
11. 蝶たち
12. 満月
13. 教師たち
14. 簡明な智慧
15. 犬や猫たち
16. 友情
17. 我々の回想する能力
18. 我々の喜ぶという力量
19. ダライ・ラマ　デズモンド・トゥトゥ[*1]　オスカル・ロメロ
20. 良心という贈り物
21. 人権と責任
22. 我々の育てるという能力
23. 女性優位
24. 天真爛漫
25. 我々の変わる能力

26. Mozart, Beethoven and Chopin.
27. The internet.
28. War resisters.
29. Everyday heroes.
30. Lions, tigers, bears, elephants and giraffes.
31. Conscientious objectors.
32. Tolstoy, Twain and Vonnegut.
33. Wilderness.
34. Our water planet.
35. Solar energy.
36. Picasso, Matisse and Miro.
37. World citizens.
38. Life.
39. The survivors of Hiroshima and Nagasaki.
40. The King of Hearts.
41. Rain.
42. Sunshine.
43. Pablo Neruda.
44. Grandchildren.
45. Mountains.
46. Sunflowers.
47. The Principles of Nuremberg.
48. A child's smile.
49. Dolphins.
50. Wildflowers.
51. Our ability to choose hope.

26. モーツァルト　ベートーベン　ショパン
27. インターネット
28. 反戦主義者
29. 日常の英雄
30. ライオン　トラ　クマ　ゾウ　キリン
31. 誠実な反対者たち
32. トルストイ　トゥウェイン　ボネガット[*2]
33. 荒地
34. 我々の水惑星
35. 太陽エネルギー
36. ピカソ　マチス　ミロ
37. 世界市民
38. 命
39. ヒロシマとナガサキの生存者
40. 心の王
41. 雨
42. 日光
43. パブロ・ネルダ
44. 孫たち
45. 山脈
46. 向日葵の花
47. ニュールンベルグの原理[*3]
48. 子供の微笑み
49. イルカたち
50. 野の花
51. 我々の希望を選ぶ能力

*1　南アフリカ、ケープタウンの前大僧正でアパルトヘイト撤廃に貢献した精神的指導者
*2　Kurt Vonnegut　アメリカで非常に尊敬されている小説家
*3　ニュールンベルグ裁判に従い国連によって採択された原理、ドイツ指導者の平和、戦争犯罪、第二次大戦における人権に対する犯罪を立証するための原理

Fukushima

After the meltdowns at Fukushima Daiichi
nothing was normal.

The people's laughter was put in a corner
and nobody thought much about it.

The people were exiled from their homes and farms
to become strangers in their own land.

The dreaded nightmare of radioactive wild boars
running free in the snow continues without end.

In Fukushima, the people suffered and suffer still.

フクシマ

フクシマ第一原発のメルトダウン以降
正常なものはなにもない

住民たちの笑いは角に押しやられ
誰もそのことについてあまり考えない

住民たちは自分の住み家や農園から追放され
自分自身の土地に馴染みのない人間になってしまった

放射能をおびた野生のイノシシたちが雪のなかを
野放図もなく駆けまわる悪夢は際限なくつづく

フクシマでは　住民たちはまだ悩みに悩んでいる

Take Three Gifts on Your Journey

Mr. President,

The word is out.

You will visit Hiroshima in May.

In Hiroshima, nuclear weapons become real.

The possibility of destroying civilization
becomes tangible.

Visiting Hiroshima is an opportunity to lead the way back
from the brink.

Take three gifts to the world on your journey: your courage,
your humanity, and a proposal to end the insanity.

Offer to convene the nuclear nine to negotiate a treaty
to eliminate nuclear weapons.

Set the world back on course.

Do it for the survivors.

And for children everywhere.

あなたの旅に三つのお土産をもっていってください

大統領

言葉は尽きている

貴方は五月にヒロシマを訪問する

ヒロシマでは核兵器は現実のものである

文明を破壊する可能性は
明白である

ヒロシマを訪問することは崖縁からの道を
戻る一つの機会だ

あなたの旅に世界に対する三つのお土産をもっていってください
　　即ちあなたの勇気
あなたの人間性　そして狂気を終わらせるための提案である

核保有九カ国に核兵器廃絶の協定を取り決める
会議を召集してください

世界を常道にもどしてください

それを原爆生存者たちのためにしてください

そしてそれを世界中の子供たちのためにしてください

ABOUT THE AUTHOR

David Krieger is a peace leader and poet. He is a founder of the Nuclear Age Peace Foundation, and has served as President of the Foundation since 1982. He has lectured throughout the United States, Europe and Asia on issues of peace, security, international law, and the abolition of nuclear weapons. He serves as an advisor to many peace organizations around the world and has received many awards for his work for a more peaceful and nuclear weapons-free world.

Dr. Krieger is the author or editor of many studies of peace in the Nuclear Age. Among his previous books are seven poetry volumes, including: *Wake Up!*; *Summer Grasses: An Anthology of War Poetry* (editor); *Never Enough Flowers: The Poetry of Peace II* (editor); *God's Tears: Reflections on the Atomic Bombs Dropped on Hiroshima and Nagasaki*; *The Doves Flew High*; *Today Is Not a Good Day for War*; and *The Poetry of Peace* (editor).

He is a graduate of Occidental College, where he received an award for creative writing and was the alumnus of the year in 2008. He also holds MA and Ph.D. degrees in political science from the University of Hawaii as well as a J.D. from the Santa Barbara College of Law.

著者紹介

デイヴィッド・クリーガーは平和指導者であり詩人である。核時代平和財団の創設者であり1982年から同財団の会長を務めている。彼はアメリカ合衆国、ヨーロッパ、アジアなどで、平和、安全、国際法、核兵器廃絶などについて講演した。世界中の多くの平和団体のアドバイザーを務め、もっと平和で核兵器のない世界をつくるための功績にたいして多くの賞を受賞している。

クリーガー博士は、核時代における平和研究の多くの書の著者であり、編集者である。すでに出版された著書としては、『目覚めよ！』、『夏の草原：戦争詩のアンソロジー』（編集者）、『花は決して充分でない：平和詩集Ⅱ』（編集者）、『神の涙——広島・長崎原爆投下についての回想』、『鳩は高く飛んだ』、『今日は戦争をするのにいい日でない』、『平和詩集』（編集者）などの七冊の詩集がある。

彼はオキシデンタル大学の卒業生であり、「クリエイティブ・ライティング」賞を受賞しているが、2008年の同窓生である。彼はまたハワイ大学から政治学のMA（文学修士）及びPh.D.（博士号）の称号を、サンタバーバラ法律カレッジから J.D.（法学博士）を受けている。

COMMENTARY

Hisao Suzuki
The Person Who Continues Writing Poems to Inspire People to Become World Citizens
On *AT THE CROSSROADS OF WAR AND PEACE*
New and Selected Poems
By DAVID KRIEGER

The pilot always believed he had done the right thing.
The President, too, never wavered from his belief.

He thanked God for the bomb. Others did, too.
God responded with tears that fell far slower

than the speed of bombs.
They still have not reached Earth.
 (From the last three stanzas of "God Responded with Tears")

David Krieger is the founder of the Nuclear Age Peace Foundation, and still serves as its president. Also, he is a poet who has published seven collections of poems. This collection of poems includes those poems selected by himself from previously published collections and some newly written poems. Reading the quoted poem, "God Responded with Tears", we are able to recognize in its simple phrase the conscience which exists among American people. Mr. Krieger's "pangs of conscience" that "God's Tears" that started to fall at the instant when the pilot dropped the atomic bomb "in the name of God" on a city where nearly 400,000 people lived still have not reached the earth is fully conveyed to readers. Conscience is supported by the common sense of values that tells us that people of countries other than America also have the innate right to live as Americans do. He continued presenting his inside criticism by using flexible and frank words about the fact that the government of the United States of America has occasionally invaded the rights of other countries' peoples following the logic of war for the profit of its own

解　説

「世界の市民」を促す詩を作り続ける人　　　鈴木比佐雄
デイヴィッド・クリーガー著　英日対訳 新撰詩集『戦争と平和の岐路で』に寄せて

パイロットは常に自分は正しいことをしたと信じていた
大統領もまた自分の信念を決してゆるがせなかった

彼は原爆について神に感謝した　他の者たちも同様だった
神は爆弾の速度よりも

はるかにゆっくりと落ちる涙で応えた
その涙はまだ地表にはとどいていない
　　　　　　（「神は涙をもって応えた」の最終三連より）

　デイヴィッド・クリーガー氏はアメリカの「核時代平和財団」の創設者であり現在も会長を務めていて、7冊の詩集を出している詩人である。本詩撰集はそれらの既刊詩集から自選された詩と最新詩篇が収録されている。引用した詩「神は涙をもって応えた」を読めば、そのシンプルなフレーズの中にアメリカ人の中に存在している良心の在りかを読み取ることが出来る。４０万人近くの都市に神の名の下に原爆を投下した瞬間に流れ出た「神の涙」は、未だ地表に届いてはいないというクリーガー氏の「良心の疼き」が伝わってくる。その良心は他国の人びとに対してアメリカ人と同じく固有の生きる権利を持っているという普遍的な価値観に裏付けられている。彼は他国民の生きる権利をアメリカ政府が第二次世界大戦中から大戦後の現在まで時に自国の利益の為に戦争の論理で侵し続けてきたことへの内部批判を、しなやかで率直

country, since the period of World War II until today. His conscience is penetrated by both the deep requiem for the victims of war upon whom bombs were dropped according to the obstinate insistence from the government of the United States of America and the belief that we should never forget those victims. The most outstanding characteristic of his poetry is his sincerity to acclaim the dignity of other countries' peoples from the heart of his heart, which is brimming over in the lines of his poems. Though he is an American, his mentality, which is full of common friendship surpassing ties with only America, makes his simplest English writing turn into profound poetic phrases. His fragrant poems, which are filled with paradox and humor, supported with sensitive technique, and which make us notice the madness of this world, show us a primarily sane world suggested by his imagination. And, unawares, the sense of the pain and anger against the realities that makes the youth of his country take part in wars and kill the people of other countries is developed. In this way, the "preciousness of peace" is calmly revived in the heart of our mind. This "preciousness of peace" surely must be a water vein reaching toward the distant future of human beings, passing through the "conscience pain" and leading us into "God's tears".

I, as a Japanese, feel the "conscience pain" regarding the deeds of both the Japanese government and the military authorities that invaded China and Asian countries during the Fifteen-Years-War. I also feel the "conscience pain" regarding their deeds which, following the attack on Pearl Harbor, enlarged the World War and deprived the world of enormous numbers of lives. I think, even generations after, we Japanese should bear the blame. I think it is very courageous to, like Mr. Krieger, visit the tragic places of another country, to meet hibakusha victims and other related persons, to give lectures, to write poems and critical articles for the purpose of the abolishment of nuclear weapons, and to criticize the acts of the government of the United States of America from the standpoint of international law. When I imagine whether I am able to go to China, Asian countries, and the United States of America and to act like Mr. Krieger or not, I realize the value of what he says and does.

On August 6, 2007 I published the Japanese version of *Against Nuclear Weapons, A Collection of Poems by 181 Poets* and in December of the same year, also published its English version. In the Preface of the English version it says, "We published this anthology of poems about atomic bombs so that we may not forget the victims of the atomic bombs

な言葉で提示し続けている。彼の良心はアメリカ政府の強弁から零れ落ちた戦争の犠牲者たちへの深い鎮魂と決して犠牲者たちを忘れてはならないという信念に貫かれている。彼の詩の最大の特徴は、他国民の尊厳を心の奥底から褒め称える誠実さが詩行から溢れ出ていることだ。このアメリカ人でありながらアメリカをはるかに超えて行く普遍的な友愛に満ちた精神性が、英語の最もシンプルな文章であるにも関わらず、彼の詩を濃厚で詩的なフレーズの言葉へと転換させてしまう。その香気ともいえる詩行は、逆説とユーモアに満ちていて、それらの鋭敏なテクニックに裏打ちされていて、この世界の狂気を気付かせて、正気である本来的な世界を想像力で示してくれる。そしていつしか祖国の若者を戦争に加担させ他国民の命を奪うことへの痛みと怒りが展開されて、私たちの心の奥底に静かに「平和の尊さ」を甦らせるのだ。その「平和の尊さ」とはきっと「良心の疼き」を経て「神の涙」に向かうはるかな人類の未来の水脈であるに違いない。

　十五年戦争で中国などアジアの国々を侵略し、アメリカには真珠湾攻撃をして世界大戦を拡大させ膨大な命を破壊した日本政府・軍部の行った行為に対して、私も日本人の一人として「良心の疼き」を感ずる。そのことは世代が変わろうが日本人は背負っていかなければならないだろう。クリーガー氏のように他国の悲劇の場所に行き、被爆者や関係者に会い講演をし、核兵器廃絶のための詩や論文を書き、アメリカ政府の行った行為を国際法の観点から批判していくことは、とても勇気のあることだ。かりに私が中国などのアジアの国々やアメリカに出向き、クリーガー氏と同じようなことができるかと考えると彼の行為や言動の尊さが理解される。

　私は２００７年の８月６日に『原爆詩一八一人集』日本語版を発行し、１２月には英語版も発行することが出来た。その英語版の序文に〈原爆詩とは、１９４５年８月６日・９日の原爆投下で犠牲となった被爆者たちを決して忘れることなく、広島・長崎で核兵器の使用を最初で最後にしなければならないと誓い、決して人類に未来永劫にわたって核兵器が使用されてはならず、２１世紀のできるだけ早めに核兵器のない地球という故郷を創り出そうとする

dropped on Hiroshima and Nagasaki on August 6 and 9, 1945. We vowed that the nuclear bombs used in Hiroshima and Nagasaki must remain the first and last nuclear weapons ever used by humankind. Nuclear weapons should be completely abolished forever. At the earliest time of the 21st century, the Earth must be made a nuclear-free home for humankind. These poems have been written, based on the philosophy rising from the tragedy of Hiroshima." It also said, "We ask all peace-loving poets all over the world to read this anthology, to get inspired by 'contagious sympathy', and to write poems against nuclear weapons for a future, enlarged edition of the anthology on a global scale." This was a call for an "atomic bombs poetry book" which would include the poets of the world of the future. Responding to that call, Mr. Krieger has sent us poems concerning atomic bombs many times. Afterward, in 2010, I published *God's Tears: Reflections on the Atomic Bombs Dropped on Hiroshima and Nagasaki*, in a combined English and Japanese version. As many hibakushas from Nagasaki appear in this poetry book, this book is still sold at the Nagasaki Atomic Bomb Museum today and visitors buy it. Mr. Krieger was asked many times by the Nagasaki Peace Organization to give lectures. Several years ago, he was invited by the Hiroshima Peace Organization to lecture in front of two hundred high school students and teachers. I also participated in it. He told us calmly how the dropping of the atomic bombs violated international law, and also told us logically about present conditions regarding both nuclear disarmament and nuclear proliferation all over the world, based on facts. At the same time, he quoted from his own poems filled with his sympathy for the pain of hibakusha. I was able to understand from his words how he embraced his respect and affection for them. At the end, he spoke with tears about how people who are from the country upon which the atomic bombs were dropped were able to accept him so kindly and tenderly. This was very impressive to me. I think he is a true 'world citizen' who has become a bridge beyond the border between Japan and the United States of America.

This collection of his poems includes the poem "At The Crossroads of War and Peace", which is the Prologue, followed by 71 other poems. I would like to quote the first and fourth stanzas from the Prologue.

「ヒロシマの哲学」に基づいて作られた詩群である〉と言い、〈この詩篇を読んで「感動の伝染性」に突き動かされたら、世界中の志を同じくする詩人たちにも原爆詩を書いて欲しいと願っている〉と将来の世界の詩人たちの詩篇を入れた『原爆詩集』の呼びかけをしたのだった。その呼び掛けに呼応して原爆詩を何度も送ってくれた詩人がクリーガー氏だった。私はその後２０１０年に彼の原爆詩を集めた『神の涙――広島・長崎原爆　国境を越えて』を日本語・英語合体版で刊行した。その詩集には長崎原爆の被爆者が多く出てくることもあり、今でも長崎原爆資料館では販売されており来館者が買い求めてくれている。クリーガー氏は何度も長崎原爆に関係する平和団体から講演に呼ばれている。また数年前には広島市の平和団体の招きで広島の高校生・教師二百人の前で講演をする機会があり、私も参加した。彼は冷静に原爆投下がいかに国際法に違反するか、また世界の核兵器の軍縮と拡散の現状を事実に即して論理的に語った。同時に自作の詩も引用しながら言葉の端々には被爆者の苦しみに寄り添う思いが満ち溢れていて、彼がいかに被爆者たちに敬意と親愛を抱いているかが理解できた。最後になぜ原爆を投下した国の自分に対してこのように優しく接して受け入れてくれるのかと、胸がつまり涙ぐみながら語ったことが今も心に刻まれている。彼こそは真に日米の国境を越えて懸け橋となった「世界の市民」なのだろう。

　本詩集は序詩「岐路の詩」と71篇の詩から構成されている。その序詩の一連目と四連目を引用する。

　　私は一篇の詩を書き
　　人類の岐路にたつ杭に打ちつけたい
　　賢明に道を選べとそれには書いてあるだろう

　　死の賛美などもうたくさん――
　　生を選び世界の市民となろうとそれには書いてあるだろう

I want to write a poem and nail it
to a stake at humanity's crossroads.
It would say: choose your path wisely.

It would say: enough homage to death—
choose life and be a citizen of the world.
It would say: be kinder than necessary.

I presume the word "Crossroads" is taken from the title of this Prologue to *At the Crossroads of War and Peace: New and Selected Poems*. He tells us the meaning of his poems by telling us that when people come to the crossroads of war and peace, this very words telling us to evade war that are written on a board nailed to a stake are his own poetry. Against a nation's propaganda which brainwashes the youth with nationalism, urging upon them a fighting spirit, and a sacred sense of war, he declares that his poem urges us to "be a citizen of the world" at the crossroads. He keenly describes the abnormal state that has dominated the world since the dropping of atomic bombs and traces the history of the nuclear weapon development race through the effects of the cold war and other conflicts that have continued in Vietnam, Iraq, Afghanistan and Syria. We are presented with the most urgent humanistic issue; the fact that we stand at the crossroads regarding whether mankind will be exterminated by atomic bombs, the greatest wholesale weapons of slaughter, or not. I hope that reading these new and selected poems will become a trigger for Americans, Japanese and all peoples in the world to be awakened to the call to "be a citizen of the world," as Mr. Krieger has called us to do. The last of the seventy-two poems is the newest one. It was written after President Obama's visit to Hiroshima was decided. In this poem, he writes. "Take three gifts to the world on your journey: your courage, /your humanity, and a proposal to end the insanity. / Offer to convene the nuclear nine to negotiate a treaty / to eliminate nuclear weapons." Probably two of the gifts Mr. Krieger hoped for were brought with the President, but the third gift, a concrete " proposal " to eliminate nuclear weapons, was not delivered to the hibakusha and to all those who have been hoping for their elimination. I hope that from now on Mr. Krieger will continue writing poems on the board nailed to the stake standing at the crossroads, urging us to bring to reality our hopes for the President's last gift, providing a deed for peace, along with our Japanese poets who are also writing poems on atomic bombs.

Tr. by Aya Yuhki

もっともっと親切であれとそれには書いてあるだろう

　この詩撰集のタイトルである「戦争と平和の岐路で」の中にある「岐路」という言葉はこの序詩から取られたのだろう。彼が詩を書く意味は人びとが「戦争と平和」の岐路に立った時に、その場所に立っている杭に打ちつけられた板に書かれた戦争を回避させる言葉こそが、自分の詩であると告げている。若者たちを愛国心や闘争心や聖戦などで洗脳し、戦争に駆り立てていく国家のプロパガンダに対して、「世界の市民」であれと「岐路」に掲げること、それが自分の詩であると断言する。彼は原爆後の世界が冷戦による核兵器開発競争の歴史になり、ベトナム、イラク、アフガニスタン、シリアなどでの絶えることのない戦争が続いている異常さを抉りだす。その大量殺戮兵器の最大のものである原爆を人類が廃棄するか、そのままにしておくかの「岐路」に立っていることが、最も緊急の人類的な課題であることを突き付ける。この詩撰集を読むアメリカ人、日本人、そして世界の国々の人びとがクリーガー氏の願う「世界の市民」に目覚めるきっかけとなることを願いたい。７２篇目の最後の詩はオバマ大統領が広島を訪問することが決まり書かれた最新の詩だ。その詩には「あなたの旅に世界に対する三つのお土産を持っていってください　即ちあなたの勇気／あなたの人間性　そして狂気を終わらせるための提案である／／核保有九カ国に核兵器廃絶の協定を取り決める／会議を召集してください」と書かれていた。彼の望んだ二つのギフト「勇気と人間性」は多分届けられたが、三つ目のギフトの核兵器廃絶の具体的「提案」は被爆者たちや核兵器廃絶を願う人びとに届けられることはなかった。彼は私たち日本の原爆詩を書く詩人と一緒にこれからも岐路に立つ杭の板に、最後のギフトである平和の行為を促す詩を書き続けるに違いない。

デイヴィッド・クリーガー 英日対訳 新撰詩集『戦争と平和の岐路で』
DAVID KRIEGER New and Selected Poems in English and Japanese
"AT THE CROSSROADS OF WAR AND PEACE"

2016年8月15日　初版発行
著　者　デイヴィッド・クリーガー
訳　者　結城 文
発行者　鈴木比佐雄
発行所　株式会社 コールサック社

〒173-0004　東京都板橋区板橋 2-63-4-209
電話 03-5944-3258　FAX 03-5944-3238
suzuki@coal-sack.com　http://www.coal-sack.com
郵便振替　00180-4-741802
印刷管理　（株）コールサック社　製作部

装丁　奥川はるみ

落丁本・乱丁本はお取り替えいたします。
ISBN978-4-86435-256-7　C1092　¥1500E

Copyright © 2016 by DAVID KRIEGER
Japanese translation by Aya Yuhki
Published by Coal Sack Publishing Company

Coal Sack Publishing Company
2-63-4-209 Itabashi Itabashi-ku Tokyo 173-0004 Japan
Tel: (03) 5944-3258 / Fax: (03) 5944-3238
suzuki@coal-sack.com　http://www.coal-sack.com
President: Hisao Suzuki